BETH WAS CRYING HARD NOW. . . .

"But *why?*" Beth demanded. "What did I do? Did he say why he wanted to break up?"

Jana hesitated, remembering Keith's words. *I just don't want to go out with her anymore.* There was no way she could tell Beth a thing like that.

"No," Jana said, assuring herself that this little lie was for Beth's own good.

"Well, didn't you ask?" Beth demanded.

Jana looked down at the ground, avoiding Beth's eyes. "It was none of my business."

"But I asked you to talk to him and find out what was wrong," she insisted, hiccuping back a tear.

Beth looked so miserable that Jana wanted to cry, too. "Well . . ." Jana offered helplessly, but she didn't know what else to say.

"Please go back and ask him," Beth implored. "Oh, Jana, you've got to find out what's wrong for me!"

THE FABULOUS FIVE

Breaking Up

BETSY HAYNES

A BANTAM SKYLARK BOOK®
NEW YORK · TORONTO · LONDON · SYDNEY · AUCKLAND

RL 5, 009–012

BREAKING UP
A Bantam Skylark Book / December 1991

*Skylark Books is a registered trademark of Bantam Books, a division of
Bantam Doubleday Dell Publishing Group, Inc. Registered in U.S. Patent
and Trademark Office and elsewhere.
The Fabulous Five is a registered trademark of Betsy Haynes
and James Haynes.*

ISBN 0-553-15873-2

Published simultaneously in the United States and Canada

*Bantam Books are published by Bantam Books, a division of Bantam Double-
day Dell Publishing Group, Inc. Its trademark, consisting of the words
"Bantam Books" and the portrayal of a rooster, is Registered in U.S. Patent
and Trademark Office and in other countries. Marca Registrada. Bantam
Books, 666 Fifth Avenue, New York, New York 10103.*

PRINTED IN THE UNITED STATES OF AMERICA

OPM   0 9 8 7 6 5 4 3 2 1

CHAPTER

1

"*G*osh, Jana, it seems so *weird* to think that you and Randy have really broken up," said Beth Barry as the two girls entered the front door of the public library on Saturday afternoon.

Jana Morgan paused inside the door and looked solemnly at her friend. Then she sighed. "It's only been a week, but if you want to know the truth, it seems weird to me, too. I know it was the best thing to do, though. And besides, I'm sure it will just be temporary."

"Right," Beth agreed, sounding as if she were trying to convince herself. "But I still can't understand why you did it."

"I explained all that," Jana replied with a trace of

1

impatience. "We've gone steady since sixth grade. Neither one of us has ever dated anyone else. How can we possibly be sure if what we feel for each other is real or just a habit? Don't you see, Beth— Randy and I need to date other people for a while."

Beth didn't answer.

Jana led the way to the main room of the library and put her notebook down beside one of the newly installed computers that had replaced the old card catalogs. She wished that Beth hadn't brought up Randy Kirwan. She was trying so hard to keep her mind off their "experiment," as they had decided to call it. They had even made a date for exactly one month from the day it started to see if they had changed the way they felt about each other. Still, as bad as she felt about not seeing Randy for an entire month, it made sense to her that they should cool their relationship for a while—especially, she thought with a chill, after the conversation she had had with her mother not long ago.

She and Randy had been to a Friday night dance in the Wakeman Junior High gym. Wakeman's own rock band, The Dreadful Alternatives, had played, and she and Randy had had a great time. After Randy dropped her off, her mother had fixed them both a cup of hot chocolate, and they had curled up on the sofa to talk.

Jana had still been feeling dreamy about her evening with Randy. "Mom, remember the story you used to tell me about how my father was such a great dancer, and how you danced until after midnight on the night you met?" she had asked.

Mrs. Pinkerton had sighed. "Yes. How could I ever forget? Your father was handsome and witty, and he simply swept me off my feet." She had gazed into the distance before going on. "I've often wished that I had dated a few other guys before I married him and found out that we were totally wrong for each other. Of course if I had," her mother had added, giving her a warm hug, "I would never have had you, and that would have been awful."

Jana had stared at her mother, thinking about Randy. She and he were years away from getting married, of course, but they had never dated anyone else. What if someday, after it was too late, they found out that *they* were wrong for each other? She knew that after the divorce her mother had had a tough time and had been awfully lonely before she met Wallace Pinkerton, and married him several months ago.

Jana couldn't explain all that to Beth any more than she could to Randy. It was just too private. Her mother had told her in confidence. The only person she had told was Christie Winchell, one of the members of The Fabulous Five. She had moved to London, England, and wouldn't tell a soul. But the story had convinced her that she had to find out for sure if she and Randy really were meant for each other.

It had taken Jana a long time to convince Randy

that they should break up and date other people. He had argued that he knew how he felt about her and didn't need to date anyone else to prove it. But she had stuck to her conviction, and sometimes she couldn't help wondering if she had made a big mistake.

"What topic did you choose?" Beth whispered from the computer next to Jana's.

Jana blinked back to the present and opened her notebook to the list of topics that Mrs. Clark, her Family Living teacher, had given to the class. They were supposed to pick a topic, research it at the library, and write a report. "Day-care centers," she replied.

"That's the same one I picked." Beth said, her face lighting up. "Hey, maybe we can share the research. That way, each of us will only have to look at half the sources."

"Good idea," said Jana.

She turned her attention back to the computer screen.

Do you wish to locate ___ subject, ___ author, or ___ title? Place an X beside your choice and press EN-TER.

Jana put an *X* beside SUBJECT and punched the ENTER key. She glanced around the room while she waited for the computer to process her choice and move on to the next selection. Her gaze swept the magazine racks, the case holding rental videos, and on to the large tables where she and Beth would sit to make notes as soon as the computer located the material they needed. An elderly man was reading a newspaper at one table. At another table a woman balanced a toddler on her knee as she copied something from a book.

Suddenly Jana froze. She felt herself go numb as she stared at a table near the window where Randy and Sara Sawyer were sitting with their heads close together over a large open book. Randy pointed to something on the page, and Sara nodded. It was obvious that they were studying together, probably working on the same Family Living report that she and Beth were. It was the first time Jana had seen Randy with someone else, and her heart felt as if it were shattering into a million pieces. And why did it have to be Sara Sawyer, of all people, who had been her friend for ages?

Jana looked closely at Sara. She was a total contrast to Jana, whose hair was dark brown and fell to her shoulders. Sara's honey-colored hair was short and curled softly around her face. Sara was athletic, and her complexion had the healthy glow of someone who spent a lot of time outdoors. Jana's heart sank. It was easy to see why Randy might like Sara.

"What's the matter?" asked Beth.

Jana couldn't take her eyes off Randy and Sara, so she nodded in their direction and heard Beth gasp.

"That jerk! It's only been a week!" Beth spat the

words out, but then she turned to Jana with huge, sympathetic eyes. "Oh, Jana! It's just awful. How can you stand it?"

"It's okay," Jana said, tears misting her eyes. "We're supposed to date other people, remember?"

Beth mumbled something Jana couldn't hear as she turned back to her computer and tried to concentrate on it. She couldn't let herself fall apart, especially not with Randy in the same room.

List the subject exactly as you would like the computer to search for it _____
Press ENTER.

Jana typed in "Day-Card Centers" and had started to press the ENTER key when she noticed her mistake. "Day-*Care* Centers, dummy," she muttered to herself. "I can't let this get to me."

To Jana's relief, by the time she and Beth had gone into the stacks and located the books they needed and brought them back to a table, Randy and Sara were gone.

"He probably saw you here and turned chicken," Beth commented.

"Beth," Jana said crossly. "You know he's supposed to be with other girls. Our experiment won't work if we don't date other people."

"Then why aren't you going out with other guys?" asked Beth.

Jana took a deep breath and let it out slowly. "I

will," she said with determination. "It's just hard to let guys know you're available. Most people don't understand why Randy and I broke up. They probably think I'm crying my eyes out and wouldn't want to go out with anybody else."

Beth was silent for a moment. Then she leaned closer to Jana and said in a confidential tone, "I think I'd die if Keith and I broke up—absolutely *die*—even though lately he has been acting like a jerk. I don't know what's wrong with him, but I can't help liking him, anyway."

Jana smiled and put a sympathetic hand on her friend's shoulder. "You're always saying how immature he is. If he's acting like a jerk, maybe that's why."

Beth nodded. "Yeah. I guess so. At least, I hope that's it."

Half an hour later the girls had copied all the information they needed and were heading for the door when Beth looked at her watch. "Do you realize that it's only two o'clock? It seems like it should be at least four."

"It is early," Jana agreed. "Want to go to the mall?"

Beth squinted out the window beside the door. "Naw. It's starting to rain, and if my hair gets wet, I'll get the frizzies. Let's go to Bumpers. It's closer."

Jana bit her lower lip. What if Randy and Sara were there?

Seeing Jana hesitate, Beth said, "Hey, we don't have to go to Bumpers. I mean, if you think you might run into Randy and Sara, we could go to my house instead."

Jana paused for another second and then lifted her chin. "No," she answered. "Let's go to Bumpers. I'm going to have to get used to seeing him with other girls. Besides, maybe there'll be some cute boys there for me."

Laughing, they dashed out into the rain and down the street toward Bumpers. The fast-food restaurant, which was named for the old amusement park bumper cars that decorated it, was full of kids from Wakeman Junior High, and rock music blasted from the old Wurlitzer jukebox in the corner.

As soon as they were inside the door, Beth whipped a mirror out of her backpack and groaned. "What did I tell you? The frizzies! You find us somewhere to sit, and I'll go into the girls' room and see if I can do something with this hair. Keith might be here, and I don't want him to see me looking like a Brillo pad."

Jana nodded and gazed around cautiously. If only the rest of The Fabulous Five were here. But Katie Shannon had gone to her grandmother's for the day, and Melanie Edwards was baby-sitting her little brother. And naturally Christie wouldn't be here. Still, Jana wished that Beth hadn't left her alone. What if Randy and Sara were here, after all? What would she say to them? How should she act? It would be so much easier if she had someone along with her to talk to. She could pretend to be so deep in conversation that she didn't notice them.

Easing her way through the crowd, Jana spotted an empty yellow bumper car and headed straight for it. Maybe if she didn't look around, she could avoid the embarrassment of making eye contact with Randy or Sara.

She let out a sigh of relief as she sank into the booth. So far, so good. Once Beth got back from the girls' room, Jana would be able to relax and look around to see if there really were any cute boys in the place.

Suddenly Keith Masterson pushed his way through the crowd and plopped down beside her. "Hey, Jana. How's it going?"

Startled, Jana hesitated an instant before answering. "Hi, Keith. I'm fine. So what's up?"

"Not much." He clasped his hands behind his head and leaned back, grinning at her. "Everything's cool."

Jana looked at him curiously. What did he want, anyway? Then she remembered that she and Beth had come in the door together. He had probably seen them and was waiting for Beth.

"Kirwan said you two broke up. Was he kidding?"

Jana shook her head. There was a funny sensation in the pit of her stomach, and she didn't trust herself to say anything for a moment. Finally she looked at Keith and said, "We just decided that we should date other kids, that's all."

"So that's why I saw him with Sara Sawyer a few minutes ago, right?"

Jana nodded. She didn't like the way the conversation was going. She certainly didn't want to talk about Randy and Sara Sawyer. Plastering a fake smile on her face, she told Keith, "Beth will be here in a minute. She just went to brush her hair."

"Whoa!" he said, sitting up abruptly and sliding out of the bumper car. "See you around."

"But aren't you even going to wait for Beth?" Jana demanded.

"Hey, what can I say?" Keith raised his arms in an exaggerated shrug. "Gotta split."

Frowning, Jana watched him rush through the crowd and disappear out the door.

CHAPTER

2

"*H*ave you seen Keith anywhere?" Beth asked when she got to the yellow bumper car a few minutes later. She was standing on tiptoe and craning her neck to see around the crowded room.

Jana cringed inwardly. She couldn't tell Beth that Keith had left the moment her name was mentioned. Besides, she reasoned, it might have been just a coincidence. Maybe he really did have to leave just then.

"He was here a minute ago, but he said he had to split," replied Jana.

"Ooooooh," said Beth, her voice sinking with her as she dropped onto the seat beside Jana. "Where did he go? Did he say?"

Jana shook her head. "He was in a pretty big

11

hurry, so it must have been important. Otherwise I'm sure he would have stayed around to see you."

"You told him I was here?" asked Beth. "And he still left?"

Uh-oh, thought Jana. I opened my big mouth again. "Well, I just said that you were brushing your hair, and he said that he really had to leave. I'm sorry you missed him."

"That's okay," said Beth. "We're going out tonight, so it's no big deal. Have you found anybody to flirt with yet? If you work fast, maybe we can double."

Jana couldn't help laughing. "No," she answered, "but I made a list of cute seventh-graders as possibilities. I'll read it to you, and you can tell me what you think."

She flipped open her notebook and pulled a folded sheet of paper out of a side pocket. "Okay. Here goes. Derek Travelstead, Tony Sanchez, Jared—"

"Hey, look over there," Beth interrupted. "The Dreadful Alternatives are sitting in that booth. Have you ever noticed that every single one of them is a hunk?" Then she added dramatically, "I mean, everyone would be impressed if you went out with one of the gorgeous members of Wakeman's own rock band!"

Jana glanced toward the booth where the four boys sat. "Yeah, they're cute all right," she admitted. "But Cory Dillon goes with Kimm Taylor, and

Craig Meachem dates Shawnie Pendergast. That only leaves Parker Donovan and Chris Burke."

"Sure, but *look* at them," said Beth. "They are totally awesome."

Jana looked at Chris and Parker again. Beth was right, of course. They were both terrifically good-looking. Parker was tall and slim with medium-brown hair and a lopsided grin that always made Jana wonder what sort of mischief he had been into. Chris, on the other hand, had dark, thoughtful eyes and a quiet smile. He's probably a very sincere person, she thought.

"But why are you in such a big hurry for me to find someone to go out with?" asked Jana. "A few minutes ago you were full of sympathy and said you'd absolutely die if you and Keith broke up."

"You're the one who thought up the experiment with Randy," said Beth. "I'm just trying to help. Hey, let's go over and talk to them, before *you* lose your nerve." She jumped up before Jana could protest and bounded across the room.

"Be-ETH, come back here!" Jana pleaded, but it was too late.

Beth had already scooted into the booth beside Craig Meachem and was talking a mile a minute. Each time she stopped for a breath, she darted a look over her shoulder, motioning with a jerk of her head for Jana to join them.

Jana let out a deep breath and sank back against the bumper car, wondering what to do. The only way I'm ever going to make this experiment work is to go out with other guys, she reasoned. Then why is it so hard even to talk to them?

Just then, out of the corner of her eye, she saw Randy. He was walking toward the order counter, but he stopped when he saw her.

Jana gulped hard and tried not to look at him, but she couldn't help it. Her eyes met his for an instant, and then she looked away. He had looked so sad that she wanted to cry.

No! she told herself. I've got to do this, or else we're right back where we started.

Picking up her notebook and jacket, Jana headed for the booth where Beth sat with The Dreadful Alternatives, noticing as she went that Randy had moved on to the counter now and was placing his food order.

"Hey, Jana," Beth called as she saw Jana approaching. Turning, she yelled, "Move over, Craig, and make room for Jana."

"There's room on this side," said Parker, flashing a big smile at Jana. "Come on. Sit down."

Jana was surprised at the flush of pleasure she felt and hoped he hadn't noticed. She gave him a quick grin and sat down beside him.

"So like I was saying," Beth said, "he was doing forty-five in a thirty-mile zone."

"Wow!" cried Cory, laughing and slapping his knee. "I can't believe it."

"Who was doing forty-five in a thirty-mile zone?"

asked Jana. She could feel Parker looking at her, and it made her nervous.

"Our beloved principal, Mr. Bell," Beth told her.

"Oh, come on," scoffed Jana. "Mr. Bell wouldn't do a thing like that."

"Oh, yeah?" countered Beth. "Marcie Bee's uncle is a policeman, and he's the one who gave Mr. Bell the ticket. Isn't that a riot?"

When Jana shook her head in disbelief, Chris chimed in, "Hey, give the guy a break. He's human."

"So I hear you and Kirwan split up," said Parker. He was turned toward Jana and totally ignoring the rest of the conversation.

Little prickles raced up the back of Jana's neck. She looked to Beth for help, but her friend was too busy with her story about Mr. Bell to notice Jana. "Uh-huh," she said softly.

"His tough luck." Parker gave her a sly grin.

Jana felt her face turn hot. She caught Beth's eye and said quickly, "It's getting late. I'd better be heading home."

Beth made a face at Jana and then sighed in resignation. "Okay. I'll go with you. See you guys later." She jumped up, started to leave, and waved back at the boys in the booth.

Jana gave them a small wave, too, and then made a beeline for the door with Beth right behind her.

"What did you do that for?" Beth demanded as soon as they were outside. "Things were just getting *interesting*. I could tell that Parker was zeroing in on you. What did he say? Did he ask you out?"

"Whoa!" said Jana. "Not so fast. I don't think I'm ready for this."

Beth put her hands on her hips and gave Jana an impatient look. "But you're the one who started it."

Jana didn't answer. It was impossible to explain to Beth how she felt. She wasn't even sure herself.

"I know!" Beth blinked her eyes open as if a light had just flashed on in her brain. "I'll call Shawnie and ask her to talk to Craig about hinting around to Parker to ask you out."

"But, Beth—"

"You guys would make a great-looking couple," continued Beth, totally ignoring Jana's protest.

Back home a little while later Jana grabbed a soda out of the fridge and took it to her room, dropping down on her bed to sip the cold drink and think.

It had been her idea for Randy and her to date others. There was no question about that. And she still believed it was the right thing to do. But why was she suddenly so nervous? And what would she do if Parker Donovan asked her out?

CHAPTER

3

"*Eeeyew!* It's green!" shouted Beth, making a face.

"What is it?" asked Jana, peering into the bowl that Katie had stuck under her nose.

The Fabulous Five had decided to get together in Jana's bedroom the next afternoon for a study and gab session, since it was too rainy out to do anything else. Only Melanie hadn't arrived yet.

"It's spinach dip," Katie said proudly. "I made it myself, and I brought it for us to eat during our meeting."

"But it's *green*," insisted Beth.

Katie put a hand on one hip and looked down her nose at Beth. "It's supposed to be green. It has spinach in it. Now that my mom has started writing a gourmet food column for the local paper, I've decided to start making some of her recipes. Here, take a cracker and try some. It's *très* gourmet."

Beth backed away. "What is *tray* gourmet?"

"*Très*," Katie repeated. "You know, French for very. This dip is *very* gourmet. Come on, guys, try it."

Jana exchanged dubious glances with Beth and tried to decide what to do. Katie's *très* gourmet spinach dip looked awful. Fortunately, at that moment, the bedroom door opened, and Melanie came rushing in.

"Hey, I got a letter from Christie!" she sang, waving an envelope in the air.

"Go ahead and read it," Jana said eagerly. "Everybody's here."

There was a catch in Jana's throat at the mention of Christie Winchell, the fifth member of The Fabulous Five, whose move to London had left a blank space in their group that was impossible to fill. Christie wrote often to her friends, addressing her letter to a different member of The Fabulous Five each time but meaning it for everyone. Jana wondered what Christie thought of her breakup with Randy and if she would mention it in this letter.

Melanie carefully turned her wet raincoat inside out and put it on Jana's bed before sitting down on the edge and pulling the letter out of the envelope. "Wait till you hear this," she said excitedly.

Dear Melanie,
Boy, the weather in London is everything you've ever heard it was. It's rained for so long that I swear I'm getting webbed feet just like a duck!

"Tell me about it," muttered Katie, glancing toward the rain-streaked window.

"Be quiet, Katie," said Melanie. "I'm getting to the good part."

I really wish you guys could meet Connie Farrell. I know that he's an umpteenth cousin to the queen, but he really doesn't act the way I've always imagined royalty would act. In fact, he's super. And he's handsome and fun. And I absolutely LOVE his beautiful horse, Rigel. The only problem is, I still like Chase!
I really wish I could talk to you and the rest of The Fabulous Five about this. You're the best friends in the world, and I miss you guys so much!
That's about all the news from here. Write soon!
Love,
Christie

Melanie let the letter flutter to the floor as she fell back against the bed, pretending to faint. "Can you imagine dating *royalty*?" she gushed, sitting back up and looking around with wide eyes. "I can just hear it now. 'Would you like to go out with me Saturday night, Christie? If you do, I'll present you to the queen.' Or maybe they'll double with Charles and Di!"

"Wow," said Jana, shaking her head. "I always knew that Christie was special, but dating royalty! That's really something."

"I can't help feeling a little sorry for Chase," commented Katie, poking a cracker into the green dip and eating it.

"Why?" asked Melanie. "Christie wrote him that she still likes him, but that she isn't sure if she's coming back anytime soon, so they should date other people."

"I know," replied Katie, "but he's really got it bad for Christie." She glanced at Jana and frowned. "Just like Randy has it bad for you."

Jana turned to Katie. "I thought you, of all people, would understand, even think it's a great idea. I thought you'd see me as sort of *liberated*, or something."

"Come on, Jana," said Melanie. "Everybody knows that you and Randy are perfect for each other. You guys will get married and live happily ever after."

Jana smiled weakly. That's what my mom expected for herself and my dad, she thought. There was no use trying to explain. There was nothing she could say without giving away her mother's secret.

Jana glanced across the room at Beth. She had

hardly said a word since Katie passed her the green dip. It wasn't like her to be so quiet.

"So how was your date with Keith last night?" asked Jana, hoping to draw Beth into the conversation.

"Don't ask," Beth muttered, and then looked helplessly at her friends. "I don't know what's wrong with him," she went on.

"What do you mean?" asked Melanie. "What happened?"

"Nothing. And I mean that's exactly what happened—*nothing*! We went to a movie at Cinema Six, and what did he do while we waited to get into the theater? He left me standing by the concession stand while he horsed around with Joel Murphy and Tony Sanchez. Then once we got inside and the movie started, he treated me as if I had bad breath or something. He leaned on the arm of the seat opposite from me and never once held my hand."

Jana frowned, remembering how Keith had left Bumpers yesterday as soon as Beth's name was mentioned. Maybe it wasn't just a coincidence, after all.

"He was probably just in a bad mood," offered Katie. When Beth gave her a puzzled look, she added, "You know. He could have had a fight with his parents, or something."

"I'm sure everything is going to be okay," Melanie said sympathetically. "You know how boys are sometimes—*weird*!"

Beth shrugged, and lapsed into silence again.

When The Fabulous Five meeting broke up later in the afternoon, Beth lingered, pretending to search her coat pockets as if she were looking for something important. As soon as the others had gone, she dropped her coat on Jana's bed and sank down beside it. "Jana, I have to talk to you. It's an emergency."

"Of course, Beth. You know you can always talk to me," Jana said gently. She could guess what was coming, and she took a deep breath and sat down beside her friend. "It's about Keith, isn't it?"

Beth nodded and looked as if she were struggling to hold back tears. "It was just awful, Jana. He didn't say six words to me all night. I tried to ask him what was wrong, but he wouldn't tell me. He just kept saying 'nothing.' But I knew that wasn't true."

"Is there anything he could be mad about?" asked Jana. "Have you done anything lately that he didn't like?" She was thinking back to the times Keith had been jealous of all the time Beth spent with the Drama Club. In fact, they had almost broken up once because he said she cared more about acting than about him.

Beth shook her head. "I can't think of *anything*, and, believe me, I've tried. Oh, Jana, I like him so much. I know we've had problems sometimes because he's immature, but he's fun and almost as crazy as I am. I'm really worried." She hesitated and then said just above a whisper, "He didn't even kiss me good-night."

Jana's hopes sank. It wasn't Beth's imagination, after all. Something really was wrong, and she couldn't stand to think of her best friend's getting hurt.

"You've got to do me a favor," Beth said earnestly. "Please, you're the only one I can ask."

Jana knew she had no choice, even though red warning lights were flashing in her brain. "What?"

"Call Keith," Beth implored. "Call him and ask him what's wrong. Just don't tell him I put you up to it."

"Oh, Beth. I don't know," she replied slowly. "I mean, what excuse could I use for calling? He knows we're best friends."

"I don't know. You'll think of something."

Jana bit her lower lip. Beth looked so miserable that she couldn't possibly say no. Finally she took a deep breath and said, "Okay. I'll try, but I can't promise that he'll tell me anything."

Beth wrapped her arms around Jana and gave her a huge hug. "Oh, thank you! *Thank you! THANK YOU!* You don't know how much better I feel already. And I'll call Shawnie about Craig's talking to Parker, too. I promise!" Beth grabbed her coat and headed for the door. "And call me the instant you talk to Keith, okay?"

Jana agreed and closed the door behind Beth. Now what am I going to do? she wondered.

She went back into her bedroom and sat down at her desk. She knew it was almost time to help her mother get supper ready, but first she had to figure out a way to talk to Keith. She opened her notebook and began scribbling down possible things to say.

Hi, Keith. This is Jana. I was wondering if I could talk to you about Beth. She paused and bit the end of her pencil. That wasn't too bad. But what next?

Are you mad at her about something? No, thought Jana, scratching that out.

Did Beth do something to make you mad? Not much better, she thought, and drew a line through the words.

Beth's a little worried that you might be mad about something, and she asked me to talk to you. Hmmm, thought Jana. That might work.

Through her closed bedroom door, she could hear the phone ringing. A moment later Mrs. Pinkerton knocked softly on the door. "It's for you, honey. A boy."

"Thanks, Mom," Jana said, and felt little tingles race across her scalp. Who could that be? she wondered. Parker? Or Randy? Gosh, I hope not. I'm not ready to talk to either of them.

Nervously she rose from the desk and went to the phone.

"Hi, Jana. This is Keith. Can I talk to you a minute?"

"Keith!" Jana exploded in surprise. "I mean, hi. I hope I didn't break your eardrum," she added apologetically. "I guess I just wasn't expecting it to be you."

"That's okay," said Keith.

There was a pause, and Jana wondered if she should ask him about Beth. Somehow the timing seemed wrong, so instead she said, "What's up?"

"Umm," fumbled Keith. "I was wondering if you'd do me a favor. I mean, a *huge* favor."

"Well . . . sure, Keith . . . if I can," she replied.

"Thanks. I knew you would."

"So what is it you want me to do?" asked Jana, puzzled.

"Tell Beth something for me," he answered.

"What?" Jana asked in surprise.

"That I want to break up with her."

Jana gasped and almost dropped the phone.

CHAPTER

4

"Keith, I can't tell Beth a thing like that!" Jana cried. "Besides, I can't believe you really mean it."

There was a loud sigh on the other end of the line, and then Keith said, "Well, I do. I can't help it. I just don't want to go out with her anymore."

Jana's mind was reeling. Poor Beth! She was going to be totally crushed!

"Well . . . well . . . why do you want me to tell her?" she asked, feeling just as confused as ever. "I'd think you'd want to tell her yourself."

"I tried to. Last night. I mean, she even asked me if something was wrong, and I chickened out."

"Well, just because you're chicken, what makes

you think I should do it?" Jana demanded. She was getting angrier by the minute.

"You're her best friend. You can say it better than I can," he offered.

"Humpf," snorted Jana.

"I mean it," insisted Keith. "Beth is a nice kid, and I know she really likes me, and—"

"Of all the egotistical things to say, Keith Masterson!" Jana shouted. "I never knew you were so conceited!"

"Come on, Jana. Let me finish."

Jana let out an angry breath, but she didn't say anything.

"I know if I try to tell her, I'll just goof it up and say it all wrong. But maybe she'll take it better if she hears it from you. Do you see what I mean?"

As badly as she hated to admit it even to herself, Jana could see his point. Keith wasn't known for being tactful. And he had been a jerk more than once since he had been dating Beth. There was no telling what he might say to her. She could be hurt twice if she heard it from him. Once by breaking up, and then by the way he said it. That would be awful, realized Jana. Maybe she should be the one to break the news to Beth, after all.

"Okay," she said slowly. "I guess maybe I could talk to her. But it's only for her sake," Jana warned. "I'm not trying to do you any favors."

"Okay, I get it," said Keith, and she could hear

relief in his voice. "Thanks a lot. And, Jana . . ." he added, "the sooner, the better, okay?"

"*Keith Masterson, you*—" But he had already hung up.

Jana put the receiver down and stomped back to her room, slamming the door behind herself. "*Now* what have I gotten myself into?" she moaned. "Poor Beth! How can I possibly tell her that Keith wants to break up with her? She'll absolutely *die*!"

A moment later her mother was outside the door. "Is everything okay, honey?" she called.

Jana sighed deeply and opened the door, motioning for her mother to come in. "First Beth wanted me to call Keith and ask him what's wrong, but before I could do that, Keith called and asked me to tell her they're breaking up."

"Wow," said Mrs. Pinkerton, shaking her head sympathetically. "How did you get in the middle of all that?"

Jana explained the whole story to her mother. "What am I going to do?"

"Well, if you want my advice, Keith really should do his own dirty work."

"But what about Beth?" Jana insisted.

Her mother thought for a moment. "I can see your point about not wanting Beth to be hurt any more than necessary, but there's no guarantee that your telling her will help much. She's still going to be hurt, and she may get mad at you for breaking the news. I'd stay out of it if I could, sweetheart. Your friendship with Beth is too precious."

After Mrs. Pinkerton left her room, Jana thought about what her mother had said. In some ways, she knew, it was good advice. Maybe it wouldn't help Beth for her to get involved. And maybe Beth would get mad at her. But at the same time, she couldn't just stand by and do nothing! Beth was her very best friend in the world.

She considered calling Melanie and Katie and asking them what they thought she should do. After all, The Fabulous Five always stuck together. But the more she thought about it, the more she knew that wouldn't work.

"Melanie would start lining up dates for Beth, and Katie would want Keith shot at sunrise," she muttered. She would just have to figure it out for herself.

Mercifully her mother didn't mention Beth while they got supper on the table or during dinner, and Pink was busy talking about the bowling tournament he was taking part in on Saturday and didn't seem to notice her quiet mood. Even while they did the dishes, her mother kept the conversation on other topics. She knows I have to make my own decision, Jana realized gratefully.

Finally, shortly after the kitchen light was turned out and her mother and Pink had settled in front of the television for the evening, Jana knew she couldn't wait any longer. She had to call Beth.

She punched in the number and listened to the ring. One. Two. Three. Four. Five.

That's funny, Jana thought as the phone continued to ring, with seven people in the family, there's almost always someone home at the Barrys'.

Jana frowned as she replaced the receiver. That meant she would have to talk to Beth at school tomorrow. They wouldn't have much privacy there. What if Beth started crying? She might have to go to class with a red nose and puffy eyes. That would be awful. Kids would ask questions, and they might guess what had happened. Even worse, Keith might see her. It would probably make his ego even bigger to see a girl cry over him.

Jana tried Beth's number three more times before she went to bed, but no one answered. There were a million places Beth and her family could have gone, of course, but knowing that didn't help. If anything, it made Jana worry about tomorrow, and she had a hard time falling asleep.

The next morning the first person she saw as she hurried to The Fabulous Five's meeting place at school was Beth. She was leaning against the chain-link fence with a mournful look on her face.

Jana's heart leapt into her throat, and she stopped in the shadows of a copper beech tree and thought the situation over. This might be a good time to break the news, since Beth was alone. But Melanie and Katie would be along any minute. Besides them, some mornings Alexis Duvall and Dekeisha Adams stood with them before school. It was just too public to tell her now.

Jana took a deep breath and stepped onto the sidewalk again.

"Hey, Jana. Come here."

She whirled around to see who had called her, knowing deep down who it had been. Keith stood a few yards away, and he was looking straight at her.

"What do you want?" she challenged.

"Come here, would you?" he insisted.

Jana sighed loudly to show her disgust and scuffed toward him. "If you want to know if I've talked to Beth yet, the answer is no. I tried to call her last night, but nobody was home."

Keith nodded that he understood and shifted from one foot to the other. "Okay," he said nervously. "But would you do it as soon as you can? I really want to get this over with."

"Oh, sure," Jana replied sarcastically. "I do this sort of thing every day. I'll just run right up to her in front of everybody and tell her you want to break up. Is that what you want me to do?"

"No, but . . . well . . ." he fumbled. "Just let me know when you've talked to her. Okay?"

Jana nodded curtly, narrowing her eyes as he walked away. "That creep!" she mumbled under her breath.

Beth's expression changed to a smile as Jana

walked toward her. Katie and Dekeisha were there now, too.

"Hi, Jana," Beth said excitedly. "I saw you talking to Keith just now. Did you ask him?" She got a mysterious look on her face, as if she didn't want Katie and Dekeisha to know what she meant, and added, "You know. The stuff we were talking about."

"Oh, that?" answered Jana. She knew immediately that her words had come out sounding fake. "Umm, well, not exactly."

Beth's face fell. "What do you mean, not exactly?"

"I can't tell you right now," Jana said quickly. "It would . . . umm . . . take too long, and the bell's going to ring."

Beth looked confused. "Well, can't you tell me what it was about?"

"I've got to hurry," called Jana, running backward toward the school. "Have to see Miss Dickinson before the bell. I'll meet you in the cafeteria at noon. Okay?"

Beth nodded as she watched Jana leave, and from the look on her face Jana knew she was already feeling hurt.

"She knows I'm hiding something," Jana whispered to herself as she hurried into the building. "And she knows I don't have to see Miss Dickinson about anything, either. Darn that Keith Masterson, anyway!"

CHAPTER

5

*J*ana was deep in thought as she headed for her homeroom, and she had almost reached room 107 when she saw Randy standing beside the door watching her approach. She caught her breath as their eyes met. She knew instantly that he was waiting for her.

She walked slowly toward him as her heart thudded in her chest. What did he want? Was he going to tell her that he liked Sara Sawyer now and was glad they had broken up?

Neither one of them said anything for a moment. Then Randy pulled a piece of paper out of his notebook and handed it to her.

"I found this and thought you might need it," he said.

Jana glanced down at the paper. It was her math homework from a couple of weeks ago. She could barely remember why she had given it to him. To check a couple of problems he had gotten wrong, if she remembered correctly.

"Umm, in case you need to study for a test or something," he added.

Jana smiled in spite of herself. There was no test scheduled in math, and even if there were, she probably wouldn't need this old homework to study for it. "Thanks," she said. "I've been looking all over for it. I'm glad you found it."

Randy glanced around uneasily, as if he were trying to think of something else to say, now that he had come up with an excuse to talk to her. Jana didn't want the conversation to end, either, and she racked her brain for something to talk about.

"I saw you at the library on Saturday afternoon." The words were out of her mouth before she could stop them, and instantly she realized what she'd done. The last thing in the world she wanted to bring up was his being with Sara Sawyer.

Randy's face colored slightly. "Yeah, we had to . . . umm . . . to work on our reports for Family Living."

Jana could feel tears gathering in a big lump in her throat and knew she wouldn't be able to force words around it, even if she tried to speak. What was she going to do now? Why had she mentioned seeing him at the library in the first place? *It was dumb!* she shouted to herself.

"Hey, would you guys move? You're blocking the door."

Jana bolted to attention. Joel Murphy was giving them a dirty look as he tried to get around them and into the classroom.

"Sorry, Joel," Randy mumbled, and stepped back out of the way.

"I guess I'd better go in, too. See you later," Jana said hurriedly, escaping into the room and to her seat before Randy could say anything else. She had to get away from him, or else she'd give away how miserable she was without him. She kept her eyes down when he came in and took his seat on the other side of the room just as the bell was ringing.

The morning dragged on, and Jana barely heard anything in any of her classes. She couldn't forget the look on Randy's face as he waited for her by the homeroom door. How can I stand to see him every day at school for a whole month until our experiment is over? she wondered.

She also couldn't help thinking about lunchtime, when she would have to talk to Beth and tell her that Keith wanted to break up. But how was she going to do that? What could she possibly say?

If only there were someone I could talk to about it, she thought. But there wasn't. She was on her own.

*   *   *

Everyone was already in the cafeteria when Jana got there. They were sitting at The Fabulous Five's favorite table. Beth munched on an apple while Katie pulled small plastic containers out of her lunch bag as if she were getting ready for a banquet. Beside her, Melanie unloaded a hot-lunch plate from her tray.

"So *now* will you tell me what you and Keith were talking about this morning?" Beth asked as soon as Jana reached the table. It was obvious from the tone of Beth's voice that she was more than a little miffed at Jana.

"Sure. As soon as we're finished eating." When Beth frowned, she added, "We'll go outside where we can have some privacy."

Beth seemed satisfied, for the moment, anyway, and Jana nibbled her cream cheese and jelly sandwich and listened to Katie explain her latest gourmet dish to Melanie.

"It's from India," Katie explained, "and the ingredients have to be mixed together at the table." She took hot rice out of a thermos and began mixing strange-looking things with it.

Jana rolled her eyes in disgust and tuned Katie out while she tried for the millionth time to plan what she would say to Beth. Her mind was blank. There just was no easy way to tell someone that her boyfriend wanted to break up with her.

Finally she couldn't put it off any longer. Lunch period was half over, and soon there might not be much privacy outside, either.

"Hey, guys," she said, turning to Katie and Melanie. "Beth and I need to talk about something. Would you mind if we went out without you?"

"'Course not," replied Melanie, and Katie agreed.

Beth looked as if she wanted to say, "It's about time," but to Jana's relief, she didn't.

They left the building, and Jana led the way across the school ground to an isolated bench. Taking a deep breath, she turned around to face Beth.

"About this morning," Jana began. "I was stalling."

When Beth's eyes got wide, Jana grabbed her friend's hand and said softly, "I just didn't want you to know, that's all."

"Know what?" Beth asked slowly, as if she were already beginning to understand.

Jana took a deep breath and cleared her throat. "I hate to tell you this, but Keith wanted me to talk to you for him and tell you that . . . that he wants to break up."

"What!" shrieked Beth. "Break up?" She looked at Jana with pleading eyes. "He didn't *really* say that, did he?"

Jana felt as if her heart would break, and all she could do was nod.

"What did he say?" asked Beth. Her voice was

shaky, and tears brimmed in her eyes. "Tell me exactly what he said. Every single word."

"Well . . ." Jana began. "When he called—"

"You mean, he called *you*?" Beth interrupted.

"Right," said Jana. "He said he wanted me to tell you that he wanted to break up. And when I asked him why he didn't tell you himself, he said that if he tried to tell you, he would probably goof it up and say it all wrong. He . . ." Jana paused and looked into Beth's tear-streaked face. "He said it might be better if you heard it from me. Oh, Beth. I'm so sorry!"

Beth was crying hard now, long sobs shaking her body. Jana put an arm around her shoulder, even though she knew it wouldn't be much comfort at a moment like this.

Beth pulled a tissue out of her jacket pocket and blew her nose, which by now was turning red. "But *why*? What did I do? Did he say why he wanted to break up?"

Jana hesitated, remembering Keith's words. *I just don't want to go out with her anymore*. There was no way she could tell Beth a thing like that. Besides, that was one thing Keith should tell her himself!

"No," Jana said, assuring herself that this little lie was for Beth's own good.

"Well, didn't you ask?" Beth demanded.

Jana looked down at the ground, avoiding Beth's eyes. "It was none of my business."

"But I asked you to talk to him and find out what was wrong," she insisted, hiccuping back a sob.

Beth looked so miserable that Jana wanted to cry, too. "Well . . ." Jana offered helplessly, but she didn't know what else to say.

"Please go back and ask him," Beth pleaded. "Oh, Jana, you've got to find out what's wrong for me! Maybe it's some little thing I did that I didn't mean to do. Or maybe it's a silly misunderstanding. Something I can fix. Don't you see? I have to know!"

Jana's mind was reeling. She knew she was getting in deeper by the minute, but there was no way she could turn Beth down. If she agreed to talk to Keith again, it would buy her a little time to figure out what to say. And maybe Beth was right about its being a silly misunderstanding or something she could fix. In fact, maybe she could talk Keith out of breaking up with Beth! There was no guarantee, but it was certainly worth a try.

"Okay," she assured her. "I'll do it."

"Oh, thank you, thank you, thank you!" shouted Beth, jumping up and down and hugging Jana at the same time. "I knew you wouldn't let me down!"

Jana tried to return Beth's smile, but deep down she had a sinking feeling that things were going to get a lot worse before they got better.

CHAPTER

6

*J*ana was heading for her locker after school when she saw Shawnie Pendergast beside the drinking fountain talking to Craig Meachem and Parker Donovan. She probably wouldn't have noticed them if she hadn't remembered her conversation with Beth at Bumpers Saturday afternoon. Beth had been excited about calling Shawnie and suggesting that she talk to Craig about the possibility of Parker's asking Jana out. Jana shook her head, thinking how ironic it was that just a couple of days ago Beth had been trying to find a way to fix her up with Parker, and now Beth didn't have a boyfriend, either.

Jana walked past them, but a moment later she heard someone call her name. When she turned to see who it was, Parker hurried toward her. Jana watched the tall eighth-grader approach, thinking that he really was awfully good-looking. But, of course, no one compared with Randy.

"Hey, Jana, could I talk to you a minute?" he asked, giving her the little mischievous grin that seemed to come so naturally to him.

Eeek! thought Jana, trying not to panic. Had Beth actually called Shawnie and suggested a fix-up between Parker and her, after all?

She took a deep breath and tried to appear calm. "Hi, Parker. Sure. What's up?"

"I just wondered if you got the history assignment." He grinned again, looking more impish than ever. "I never can keep my mind on what Mr. Naset is yakking about up there. I mean, history is one *boring* subject."

"Yeah, I got it," Jana replied, hoping the relief she felt didn't show on her face. "We're supposed to read chapter seventeen and answer the questions at the end."

Parker made a note on the cover of his notebook with a stubby pencil, which he stuck behind an ear. "Gotcha," he said, and fell in step beside her. "Chapter seventeen. Answer the questions. Oughta be a breeze."

Jana nodded. Why was he walking with her? she wondered. Why didn't he just go on about his own business?

"Come to think of it, it probably won't be much of

a breeze," said Parker. "No matter how many times I read those history chapters, I don't have much luck with the questions."

"Maybe you just don't concentrate when you read," Jana offered. She certainly had no intention of letting him copy her answers, if that was what he was getting at.

"That's probably it," agreed Parker. "I need someone right there with me, reminding me to concentrate."

Jana wondered briefly if she should say, Yeah, maybe your mom could do it. But Parker wasn't finished talking.

"How about if I come over tonight, and we can study together. I won't copy your answers," he said quickly, holding up his hands in mock surrender. "I promise. And then, after we get all this boring history stuff out of the way, we can go to Bumpers for a little while. Lots of kids go during the week."

Jana could hear her pulse pounding in her ears. Here it was. The moment she had been both looking forward to and dreading. The moment another boy asked her out. She swallowed again. Her ears were ringing now. She couldn't possibly go out with Parker. How would she act? What would she say? But if she didn't, she reminded herself, hers and Randy's experiment would never have a chance to work. Besides, fewer kids went out on school nights than on weekends, which meant fewer would see her out with someone besides Randy. *Randy*. His name echoed in her mind, and she knew it was really Randy she was worried about. She didn't want him to see her with another boy.

"I guess that would be okay." The words sounded thin as she pushed them out of her mouth. She looked up at Parker, who suddenly seemed taller than ever. He was grinning his mischievous grin. "Come over about six-thirty," she added.

"Great. I'll be there." Parker ducked away toward his own locker, leaving her standing in the middle of the hall with weak knees.

She had done it! She had accepted a date with another boy! *For tonight!* "Oh, my gosh," she murmured as she hurried to her locker. Her hands were trembling so much that it took three tries to work the combination.

Jana had just come into her apartment and was still in a daze from accepting a date with Parker Donovan when the phone rang.

"Have you talked to him?" Beth demanded the instant she said hello.

"Who, Parker?" Jana asked, then realizing that wasn't who Beth meant at all, she said quickly, "I meant Keith. No, I haven't had a chance yet."

Beth's voice fell. "Oh," she said. "Well, when are you planning to talk to him? Oh, Jana, things were going so much better between us until just lately. I've got to find out what's wrong so that I can patch it up."

Jana looked up at the ceiling helplessly. What was she going to say? So much had happened today that she hadn't had time to plan when she would talk to Keith.

"How about tonight?" Beth continued. "You could call him after supper."

"Can't," Jana told her. "Parker Donovan is coming over to study history. Then we're going to Bumpers."

"Great," said Beth without much enthusiasm. "I guess Shawnie must have talked to Craig about Parker. I hope you guys have fun."

Jana felt a rush of guilt. Beth had called Shawnie, and now Jana had a date while her best friend was wallowing in misery. Even if she confessed to Beth how nervous she was about going out with Parker, it wouldn't help.

"I'll call Keith right now," she promised. "And if he isn't home, I'll keep calling until Parker gets here. Okay?"

"Thanks, Jana," said Beth gratefully. "You're the best friend anyone could ever have."

After she hung up the phone, Jana gazed around the empty apartment. It would be another hour before her mom and Pink got home from work. It would be best to call Keith now, the way she had promised, while there was no one around to hear her conversation. But what am I going to say? she asked herself as she punched in his number. It was too late now to make plans. She would just have to play it by ear. Who knows, she thought hopefully, maybe he won't even be home.

Naturally Keith answered the phone.

"Hi, Keith," said Jana.

"Hey! Jana!" he cried, and she couldn't help thinking that he seemed surprisingly glad to hear her voice.

"Listen, Keith. There's something I need to talk to you about," she said. "It's about Beth," she added softly.

"Oh, yeah. I saw you talking to her at noon. She looked pretty torn up."

Jana was irritated that he sounded so unconcerned, but she didn't say so. Instead, she went on, "I was wondering about why you broke up with her. I know you said that you just got tired of going with her . . ." Jana hesitated, gathering courage, and then plunged on. "But I was wondering if there was another reason. You know, maybe something she did that you didn't like. Or something she said."

There was a pause on the other end of the line. "Now that you mention it, there was another reason," he replied.

Jana's hopes leapt. "There was?"

"Sure," Keith answered, sounding pleased again. "A big reason."

"Could you tell me what it was?" Jana asked. "You see, Beth still really likes you, and if it was a misunderstanding or something like that, maybe you guys could get back together."

"Naw," Keith assured her. "It's nothing like that."

"Are you certain?" Jana pressed. "Maybe she could explain, or even apologize. Are you sure it wouldn't work?"

"Positive," said Keith. "And if you really want to know why I broke up with Beth, I'll tell you."

"Okay," Jana murmured, waiting tensely.

"So that I can ask you out now that you and Randy have split."

Jana's mouth dropped open in horror. "What?" she whispered.

"You heard me. It's you I like, not Beth. I've liked you for a long time, but I knew I didn't stand a chance while you were going steady with Kirwan."

Oh, no! thought Jana. This can't be happening. *What am I going to tell Beth now?*

CHAPTER

7

Jana couldn't believe what she was hearing. The last thing in the world she wanted was to be the cause of Beth and Keith's breaking up.

"I have to go now. My mom's calling me," she lied.

As soon as she hung up the phone, she sprawled across the sofa and buried her face in one of its soft cushions. What's happening? she asked herself over and over.

It had started out so innocently, with her deciding that she and Randy should date others for a while to see if they really cared for each other as much as they believed they did. And they had made a date for one month after the breakup to talk things over.

That was it. No big deal. But now, Beth had a broken heart because Keith had broken up with her, and Keith wanted to take Jana out.

"Beth will hate me if she ever finds out," Jana whispered. "My very best friend in the world will never trust me again."

Jana was still lying on the sofa when her mother came home a little while later. "Something wrong, dear?" Mrs. Pinkerton asked.

Jana poured out the whole story for her mother, and was grateful when she didn't say, I told you so. Instead Mrs. Pinkerton gave Jana a sympathetic pat and said, "I wouldn't worry too much. I'm sure you don't intend to go out with Keith, do you?"

"Of course not," said Jana. "I wouldn't go out with him if he were the last boy on earth."

"Then how could Beth get mad at you? You can't help it if Keith has a crush on you. Beth may not be happy about it, but she can't blame you," Mrs. Pinkerton assured her.

Jana felt a little better, and by the time six-thirty came, she was actually looking forward to getting to know Parker better. It was exciting that he was part of a rock band, and he definitely was handsome. Still, she was awfully nervous.

Maybe I can talk him out of going to Bumpers after we finish our homework, she thought, since being seen in public with him is the scariest thing of all. We could watch TV or something instead.

She almost jumped out of her skin when the doorbell rang.

"Do you want to get that, Jana?" called Pink from the living room. "It's probably your friend."

Jana raced to the door and opened it. Parker was standing there with his books in hand, grinning as usual. She ushered him into the apartment's tiny foyer. "This is my mom and my stepdad. Mom and Pink, this is Parker Donovan."

"Hi, Parker. Welcome," Pink said, shaking Parker's hand while Jana's mother said hello.

"Hello, Mr. and Mrs. . . . umm . . ."

He looked helplessly at Jana, and she realized that he didn't know their last name.

"Pinkerton," she said quickly. Of course he wouldn't know, she thought. This is the first time he's ever met them. But still it seemed strange. She had never had to clue in Randy about anything like that. He had been around long before her mom and Pink had gotten married.

"So do you like to bowl?" Pink asked Parker, his voice full of enthusiasm. Parker was glancing at the shelf full of bowling trophies in the living room.

"Never tried it," answered Parker.

"Well, one of these days . . ." Pink began, but Jana's mother cut him off.

"I'm sure Parker has lots of things to keep him busy," she said gently to her husband, and then winked at Jana. "Make yourself at home, Parker."

Then she steered Pink back to the living room, where the television was on.

Jana led Parker into the kitchen and stood there awkwardly for a moment. "I guess we can study in here," she said, gesturing toward the table.

"Sure." He dropped his books on the side of the table nearest the refrigerator and sat down.

Jana frowned. Randy always sat on the other side when they studied together. Not that it mattered. Except that the kitchen was tiny, and if Parker sat next to the fridge, she would have to ask him to move when she got out sodas and ice. Sighing, she got her own books from the counter and placed them across the table from Parker.

"Want something to drink before we get started?" she asked brightly.

"Sure," he said. "Got any root beer?"

Jana shook her head. Randy always drank cola. "All we have is cola," she told him apologetically.

"Naw," he replied. "I'll just skip it."

Jana swallowed hard. Why hadn't she thought to get something besides cola on her way home from school? She should have known Parker might want something else. Not every boy was like Randy.

The thought made her sit up straight. Then she slumped again. Of course every boy isn't like Randy, she scolded herself.

"I'll go ahead and start the popcorn, then," she said. She and Randy always ate popcorn while they studied, and everybody in the world liked popcorn.

"Hey, don't make any for me." Parker grinned. "I love the stuff, but it gets under my retainer."

"Oh," Jana said, feeling totally deflated. "Is there anything you would like?"

Parker thought a minute. "I forgot my pencil."

Jana grabbed an extra pencil out of the cup beside the phone and handed it to him. "I guess we'd better get started," she said with the best smile she could muster.

Parker nodded. "Yeah, the sooner we get started, the sooner we get it over with." Then he grinned and added, "And we can cut out for Bumpers."

Jana sat down and opened her history book, flipping to chapter seventeen. She looked nervously across at Parker, who was slowly turning the pages of his book. He looked so relaxed, and her heart was thumping away like a runaway bumper car. He didn't like cola. He couldn't eat popcorn. And he was in a big hurry to get to Bumpers, where tons of Wacko kids might see them. Things weren't going well at all, and she didn't know what to do about it.

She jumped a foot when the phone rang. She heard her mother answer. A few seconds later she appeared in the kitchen doorway. "It's Beth."

Jana felt goose bumps rise on her arms. Beth must be feeling pretty desperate to be calling now. Jana *had* promised Beth she would call her as soon as she talked to Keith, but Beth knew that Parker was coming over to study.

"Would you explain that I can't talk to her now?"

Jana asked, nodding toward Parker, who was bent over his book, tapping a beat on the table with his pencil while he read.

Her mother nodded and left the room. Jana felt bad about not talking to Beth. But what could she do? Even if she knew what to say to Beth, which she didn't, she certainly couldn't say it in front of Parker.

She went back to her reading, but she wasn't making much progress. In fact, she realized, she had just read the same paragraph three times.

Suddenly Parker looked up at her. His eyes were twinkling, and he gave her a lopsided grin. "Hey, that's enough reading. I can't hack any more of this stuff! Let's start on the questions."

Jana was dumbfounded. "But how can we answer the questions if we haven't read the chapter?"

Parker shook his head in amusement. "We'll look up the answers. That's all we need for the test, anyway."

"But—" sputtered Jana.

"I know what I'm talking about," said Parker. He leaned back in his chair and gave her a cocky grin. "Old Naset always uses the questions at the end of the chapters for his tests. He'd never go to the trouble of making up his own. Reading the chapter is just a waste of time."

Jana wasn't sure how he talked her into it, but half an hour later they had looked up the answers to all the history questions and were walking into Bumpers. Loud music came from the old Wurlitzer jukebox, and the place was filled with an astounding number of kids that Jana knew.

"Now this is what I call homework!" Parker exclaimed happily as he steered her toward a table near the front door. But instead of sitting down with her, he began gyrating to the rap beat of the song and lip-synching the words.

Jana wished she could crawl away somewhere and hide. So what if he was one of The Dreadful Alternatives? Did he have to put on a solo performance when she was there with him!

Kids in nearby booths clapped their hands in time with the music and urged him on. Others moved closer from booths farther away. It was obvious to Jana that Parker was loving every minute of it. "*All RIGHT!*" he yelled as the music ended and everybody applauded wildly.

Parker made a little bow to the crowd and sat down, spinning around to give Jana a dopey grin.

She tried to smile back, but her face felt like cement. She was glad when she heard someone call her name.

"Hi, Jana!" Dekeisha Adams sped across the floor, carrying a plate of french fries. "See you're with Mr. Cool!" she added behind a hand, and then giggled.

Before Jana could answer, Alexis Duvall yelled from a booth, "Hey, Morgan. What are you doing here on a school night?"

Jana waved to both Dekeisha and Alexis. Mr.

Cool, Dekeisha had called Parker. Jana frowned. I'd like it better if he were a little less cool, she thought.

"Isn't this place great?" Parker asked, drumming his fingers on the table. "It's always like this on school nights. You don't know what you've been missing by staying home and reading your history book," he added, raising an eyebrow.

She felt a tap on her shoulder and looked around to see Alexis standing there.

"Want to go to the girls' room with me?" asked Alexis. "I need to talk to you."

Jana excused herself and followed Alexis, grateful to get away from Parker for a moment. When they reached the restroom, Alexis looked around and didn't speak until she was sure they were alone.

"I just wanted you to know that Randy's here," she said.

Jana gulped. "He is?" she asked weakly. "Is he with anyone?"

Alexis nodded. "He came in with Tony Sanchez, but half the girls in the place are sitting in their booth and flirting their heads off with Randy. And he's loving every minute of it."

"Who's flirting with him?" Jana demanded.

"Laura McCall and Tammy Lucero were there for a while. Now Marcie Bee and Melinda Thaler are sitting there, and naturally Sara Sawyer. She told Lisa Snow that she's had a crush on Randy for ages and that she's thrilled you guys broke up."

"You're kidding!" Jana exploded. "Sara Sawyer's supposed to be my friend!"

"Ha!" scoffed Alexis. "You know as well as I do that friendship goes down the tubes when it comes to boys. If you ask me, you should never have let Randy out of your clutches."

At that moment Jana couldn't have agreed more.

CHAPTER

8

*J*ana glanced toward Randy's booth as she left the restroom. Alexis had been right. Not only were Marcie and Melinda sitting with Tony and Randy, but Sara was right beside him, looking at him with adoring eyes. What was worse, Randy was smiling back at her.

Pain stabbed Jana's heart. She couldn't stand to look at them, so she took a deep breath and hurried back to the table where Parker waited.

His face lit up as she approached. "I got us a couple of root beers," he said, waving a hand toward a pair of glasses on the table.

Jana tried not to frown. Why hadn't he asked her what she wanted instead of going ahead and get-

ting her something? She hated root beer! Randy
would have brought her a cola, *after* he had asked her
what she wanted. *He* was totally considerate, which
was more than she could say for Parker.

She sighed and sat down, murmuring thank you.
Then she picked up the glass and put the straw in
her mouth, taking a tiny sip of the sickly sweet root
beer. At least that way, she could avoid talking. Parker was really getting on her nerves.

"I'd better be heading home," she said a few minutes later.

"Hey," protested Parker, "we just got here."

"I know, but I forgot that I have some other homework to do," she lied, hoping that he wouldn't ask
her which subject.

Parker shrugged and loudly slurped the last of his
root beer. Jana cringed in embarrassment. Randy
would never do a thing like that.

She darted a quick look toward Randy's booth as
she and Parker left Bumpers. Her heart sank. Sara
was still looking at Randy adoringly. Randy was still
smiling at her. And now they were alone in the
booth.

Parker talked a mile a minute as they walked back
to Jana's apartment building. He told her about the
new songs The Dreadful Alternatives were working
on and about a date they had in two weeks to play
for a ninth-grader's birthday party.

Jana nodded a few times at appropriate places, but
otherwise she was glad that she didn't have to make

conversation. She was anxious to get this evening over with. Parker Donovan was *definitely* not the boy for her.

When they reached her front door, Jana thanked him for the root beer at Bumpers and started to say good-night as she dug in her jacket pocket for her key.

Suddenly Parker bent toward her, slipping one arm around her and lifting her chin with his other hand. Before she knew what was happening, he kissed her so hard on the lips that she could feel the outline of his retainer.

Her eyes opened wide as she pushed away from him, but if he knew she didn't like the kiss, he didn't show it.

"Gotta go now," said Parker, his impish grin re-appearing. "Catch you later."

Jana sank against the door and watched him disappear down the hall.

"So how did things go with Parker Donovan last night?" Melanie asked Jana. Melanie and Katie were already standing by the fence when Jana arrived at school the next morning.

Jana blew out an exasperated breath before she answered. "He's such a show-off. We went to Bumpers, and he made an idiot of himself lip-synching to a rap song. You wouldn't believe how embarrassed I was." She couldn't bring herself to tell them about the kiss.

"You're just not used to guys like him" said Melanie. "After all, he's always on stage."

"You can say that again," muttered Jana.

"Let's face it, there's nobody like Randy," added Katie. "I don't think you guys should have broken up."

"Randy was at Bumpers, too, with Sara Sawyer," Jana told them, frowning at the memory. "Alexis said that Sara's glad we broke up because she's had a crush on Randy for ages."

Katie and Melanie exchanged glances. "We heard that, too," said Katie. "She told Marcie Bee that she's going to ask Randy to go skating this weekend. According to Marcie, Sara skates on roller blades, and she is FAN-TAS-TIC!"

Jana sighed. "I tried on a pair of roller blades once, and I couldn't even stand up on them. What's worse, Randy admires athletic people, and he'll probably think Sara is terrific."

"Don't be silly," insisted Melanie. "It's you Randy likes, and you know it."

Jana didn't answer. Instead, she glanced at her watch. Beth should be here any minute, she thought, but she still hadn't decided what she was going to say. I guess I'll just have to wing it. Jana looked around to see if Beth was coming yet, but instead of Beth, she saw Keith heading their way.

When he saw her glance at him, he started to trot, yelling, "Hey, Jana. Can I talk to you a minute? It's important."

Jana hesitated. She really didn't want to talk to Keith.

"What do you suppose he wants to talk to you about?" asked Katie.

"Maybe he's changed his mind about breaking up with Beth," Melanie said breathlessly.

Was that possible? Jana wondered. If it was, it could be the best news she'd heard in a long time. "I'd better go find out," she said to her friends, and then hurried toward Keith.

"What is it?" she asked hopefully.

Keith fidgeted nervously. "You know what I was talking about on the phone?" he asked.

Jana nodded, holding her breath.

"Well . . . well, I just wondered if you'd go to a movie with me on Friday night."

"What?" Jana shrieked. "Keith Masterson, you know very well that Beth is my best friend!" She stopped, realizing for the first time how loud she was talking. Several kids had stopped to look at her and Keith. Stepping closer to him, she continued in a lower tone. "I couldn't go out with you even if I wanted to."

He moved toward her. "That doesn't make any difference."

Jana was getting flustered. "Of course it does," she insisted. "I can't just . . . just . . ." Suddenly she was aware that Keith was staring at something over her left shoulder. She frowned and waited for him to look at her again. When he didn't, she turned slightly to see what he was so interested in. It was Beth.

Beth was standing with Katie and Melanie. She was watching Jana and Keith with a hopeful expression on her face. Oh, no, thought Jana. Beth thinks maybe I'm patching things up between her and Keith. If she only knew.

"I've got to go now," Jana muttered to Keith. She didn't wait to hear his reply. Instead she headed slowly in Beth's direction. At that same moment Beth started walking toward her. Jana could see Melanie and Katie leaning against the fence, watching, too.

"So what did you find out?" Beth asked anxiously when they met. "Did Keith tell you why he broke up with me? Is it something stupid that I did? Something I can fix?"

Jana tried to act casual. "Gosh, I'm not sure."

Beth looked puzzled. "What do you mean, you're not sure? What did he say?"

Jana knew it was useless to stall. The important thing was to keep Beth from finding out the truth. She took a deep breath.

"He just doesn't want to go steady anymore." The words almost stuck in her throat. Still, she had started the lie; she had to finish it. "You know what copycats boys are. Just because Randy isn't going steady, Keith doesn't want to, either."

"Is that what he said?" Beth asked in amazement.

Jana hedged. "Not exactly," she fumbled. "I mean, not in those words, but I'm sure that's what he meant."

"But what *did* he say?" Beth insisted.

Jana felt trapped. Why did Beth have to keep pressing? But deep down she knew that she would do the same thing if it had been Randy who had broken up with her so mysteriously. Still, what could she say to Beth? Lying was always so much harder than telling the truth.

"I don't remember his exact words. Honest," she said.

"Well, maybe you could talk to him again," Beth offered.

Jana gasped. "Again?"

"Sure," said Beth. "Maybe you could tell him that we don't have to go steady if he doesn't want to. That way we could still go out."

Beth had such a hopeful look on her face that Jana was tongue-tied. She wasn't getting anywhere at all.

"Would you do it?" Beth asked in a small voice.

"I don't think it would be a good idea."

"Why not?" Beth demanded.

"Um, I just think you ought to play hard to get," Jana said quickly, thankful for the sudden inspiration.

Beth looked skeptical. "But he knows I like him. What good would it do to play hard to get?"

"You know how guys hate to be chased," said

Jana. "I mean, if you act as if you don't care, he might get worried."

"Do you really think so?" asked Beth. "I mean, you don't think he'd just forget about me and start dating other girls, do you?"

Jana took a deep breath. "I think it's worth a try. I *really* do."

"Well . . ." Beth hesitated and looked at Jana nervously. "I guess if you say so . . . I could *try*."

"Terrific." Jana squeezed Beth's hand. She was grateful when the first bell rang an instant later, and they headed toward the school.

CHAPTER

9

*J*ana was concentrating on working her locker combination when she heard snatches of conversation coming from the direction of the lockers across the hall from hers.

". . . cutest boy in Wacko . . . didn't think they'd ever break up . . . Jana didn't know how lucky she was."

Jana's hand froze on the lock. She didn't have to turn around to know who was talking. It was Sara Sawyer, and she was talking about Randy. Jana closed her eyes and listened harder.

"So did he invite you to go to Bumpers with him last night, or did you just *happen* to see him there?" asked Lisa Snow.

Both girls giggled, and then Sara said, "It wasn't a date. I overheard him talking to Tony Sanchez in math class yesterday. They were making plans to go to Bumpers, so *naturally* I had to be there."

It sounded awful to hear someone else talk about Randy. *Her* Randy. At least he hadn't asked Sara to go to Bumpers with him. She had just shown up.

"Of course I sat with him," Sara added confidently, "and then he walked me home. I wouldn't be surprised if he asks me out for this weekend."

"All *right*!" Lisa cried.

Then they moved down the hall, and Jana couldn't hear any more of their conversation. *Randy had walked Sara home. Then he must like her!* Jana leaned her forehead against the locker, trying to ease the panic that was spreading through her. The metal felt cool, but she knew that in a minute she would have to open her locker, get her books, and go to class as if nothing were wrong. How could she do that? How could she pretend, when everything in the world was wrong?

She managed to move through her morning classes in a fog. A couple of times she spotted Parker in the hall, and she ducked behind whoever was walking in front of her to keep from being seen. The rest of the time all she could think about was Randy's having walked Sara Sawyer home. Had he kissed her good-night? The thought made her furious. Randy was *her* boyfriend! Sara had no right trying to steal him!

She was still angry when she got to the cafeteria and plopped her lunch bag down on the table where the rest of The Fabulous Five were already seated.

Immediately Katie picked up a wide-mouth thermos and a plastic spoon and held them out to Jana. "Here, try some of this. It's taco soup; I made it last night. It has chili beans and taco seasoning in it, and you eat it with corn chips. I brought some of those, too."

Jana glanced at the thermos, but she didn't take it. She wasn't in the mood for another one of Katie's crazy concoctions.

"It's yummy. You ought to try it," said Beth.

Melanie nodded. "It's the best thing she's made."

Still, Jana didn't reply.

"What's wrong with *you*?" asked Beth, putting her fork down on her hot-lunch tray and looking at Jana in amazement. "I hate to say this, but you look awful."

Tears spurted into Jana's eyes. "It shows, huh?"

"Gosh, yes," answered Katie, and Melanie nodded.

Jana tore open her lunch bag and stared at her cream cheese and jelly sandwich. It was her absolute favorite, but today the sight of it made her want to throw up. "It's Sara Sawyer," she finally said. "She's talking about Randy as if she owned him!"

She repeated the conversation she had heard at her locker. "All I can think about is Randy's walking

Sara home, and I keep wondering if he kissed her."

Katie put down her thermos of soup and looked at Jana. "If you want my advice, you'd better tell Randy you've changed your mind about breaking up before it's too late."

"That's just it," Jana protested. "I'm crazy about Randy. He's the only boy in the world for me. But if we don't go all the way through with this experiment, I may never know if he really cares about me. I mean, it certainly didn't take him very long to find a new girlfriend!"

"I think you're absolutely crazy," muttered Melanie. "I would never, *ever* take that kind of chance with Shane."

Katie nodded. "For once, when it comes to boys, I agree with Melanie. I'd hate to break up with Tony, either, for *any* reason."

"But . . . it's just that . . ." Jana sputtered. How could she explain that she had never expected Randy to find a new steady girlfriend? That she had really believed they would each go out with two or three new kids and then get back together, knowing for certain that they were really meant for each other? Now she wasn't so sure about how Randy felt. That made their experiment more important than ever.

"I think you ought to talk to him right now," said Katie.

"And just think, maybe if you guys get back together, Keith and I will, too," offered Beth with a big grin. "After all, he told you that he didn't want to go steady because Randy wasn't doing it."

Jana blinked in surprise. Beth might have a point. Keith had broken up with Beth so that he could ask Jana out, but if she and Randy got back together, Keith would have to give up on dating her. Maybe, just maybe, he might go back to Beth.

But there was no guarantee. And besides, that wasn't what the breakup was about.

Jana shook her head. "I'll have to think about it." Then looking at Beth, she added, "You know I'll help you if I can, but I'm just not sure that's the right thing to do."

A gloomy silence fell over the table until Katie broke it by asking, "Did any of you sign up to be Book Buddies for the read-in and sleepover at the public library this weekend?"

"The what?" echoed the others.

Katie shrugged and grinned. "I guess not, if you don't even know what I'm talking about. There's a notice on the main bulletin board explaining that the elementary schools have been running a contest for reading. Any second-grader who reads twenty books is eligible to go to a read-in and sleepover at the public library this Saturday night. They're going to be reading books, playing games, and having refreshments—naturally. Then the next morning they'll have breakfast and then go home."

"Sounds like lots of fun if you're a second-grader,"

said Beth. "There might even be some kids there that we know from Mark Twain Elementary."

"Right," agreed Jana. "Why do they need us?"

"Yeah," said Melanie. "What's this Book Buddy stuff you mentioned?"

"The library is looking for kids from Wakeman to go along and read to the kids, help with games and refreshments, and things like that. There'll be regular adult chaperones. They just want us to pair up with kids and help them have fun."

"Are you signing up?" Jana asked Melanie.

Melanie shook her head. "I have a date with Shane."

"I can't, either. Tony's coming over for gourmet pizza," Katie announced proudly. "Otherwise I would."

Jana sighed, remembering the times she and Randy had shared pizza. They always had pepperoni, green pepper, and mushroom—her favorite—which was gourmet enough for them. But that seemed like ages ago, and she certainly didn't have a date with him now. "I guess it might be better than doing nothing."

"Right," Beth added glumly. "I'll sign up if you will."

Jana thought for a minute. For the experiment to work, she actually should be trying to find someone else to go out with. But *not* Parker Donovan! she thought emphatically. And *not* Keith Masterson!

And right now she couldn't think of another boy who might be interested in asking her out.

"Okay," she said, sighing deeply. "We'll go sign up right after lunch."

Jana nibbled on her sandwich, feeling more depressed than ever. Entertaining second-graders all night at the public library, she thought. What a rotten way to spend Saturday night.

CHAPTER

10

*J*ana Morgan and Beth Barry were the first two names on the sign-up sheet for the library sleepover, but by the next day lots of kids were talking about it.

"It's going to seem *weird* spending the night in the public library," said Lisa as a group of girls stood at the mirror in the girls' room between classes.

"Spooky, you mean," replied Jana. "That place is always so quiet."

Beth cackled devilishly, rubbing her hands together and rolling her eyes at the others. "And at night ghostly shadows will creep out of the rows and rows of silent books and—"

"Stop that, Beth," cried Dekeisha. "You're giving me goose bumps."

"Me, too," said Lisa. "Maybe I'll take my name off the list."

"Hey, I was only joking," Beth told them. "I haven't checked the list today. Have a lot of kids signed up?"

"Quite a few," Alexis answered. "Even some boys."

Jana's hairbrush stopped in midair. Was Randy one of them? She didn't want to ask Alexis because she knew that if she mentioned Randy's name, everyone would want to talk about their breakup. She slipped her brush into her backpack and motioned to Beth that she was leaving. "Gotta run," she called, and hurried into the hall. She knew it was silly, but she just had to check the sign-up sheet to see for herself if Randy was one of the boys on the list.

It was almost time for the bell to ring, and she increased her speed to a jog as she neared the main hall, where the bulletin board was. She jerked to a halt when she rounded the corner and saw Keith coming her way.

His face lit up when he saw her. "Hey, Jana, guess what?" He didn't wait for her to reply. "I just signed up to be a Book Buddy at the library. I saw your name on the list, so I decided I'd do it, too."

Jana smiled weakly, and her mind raced. "Gosh, Keith. Are you sure you want to do something like that? It's going to be a lot like baby-sitting, you know."

Keith gave her a surprised look, so Jana decided to lay it on thick.

"Yeah, you know how second-graders are," she went on. "They'll try to get away with murder. We're really going to have our hands full. Probably half of them will eat too many cookies and throw up, and *we'll* have to clean it up."

Keith looked slightly nauseated himself for an instant. Then he shook his head and said, "Naw, they won't make us do that. There are going to be a bunch of parents and teachers there, too. *They'll* have to clean it up."

Jana frowned. "You didn't really sign up because I did, did you?"

"Sure. Why not?"

"Lots of reasons," Jana said emphatically. "For one thing, Beth's going to be there. And second, I told you that I'm not going to go out with my best friend's boyfriend, so you might as well give up."

"*Ex*-boyfriend," Keith corrected her. "And besides, you can't let Beth run your life."

Jana glared at Keith. "She doesn't run my life. She—"

The ringing bell broke into the conversation. Keith gave her a flirty grin as he turned to leave, and said, "See you Saturday night."

Jana let out an exasperated sigh and trudged to her own class, realizing later that she hadn't looked at the list to see if Randy's name was on it.

She was at her locker after school when Beth came running up.

"Jana, guess what? Keith is going to the library overnight! His name's on the sign-up sheet. Isn't that super? Maybe he saw my name, and that's why he signed up. Do you think that's it? Maybe he wants to get back together."

Jana could hardly stand to look into her best friend's eyes. Poor Beth, she thought. How would she feel if she knew the truth? How would she feel about *me*? Jana wondered, and blinked.

"Well, what do you think?" Beth insisted. "You know how nutty Keith can be sometimes. I'll bet he wants to wait until all the little kids are asleep and then get me in a dark corner of the library and ask me to get back together. Don't you?"

"Gosh," fumbled Jana. Then she shrugged and added, "You know him better than I do."

"Yeah," said Beth. She had a dreamy look on her face. "Wouldn't that be romantic?" Then she jolted to attention and grabbed Jana's arm. "I almost forgot. Randy's name is on the list, too, but—get this—Sara Sawyer's name is right under his."

Jana's heart almost broke in two. They must have signed up together. Pictures raced through her mind of Randy and Sara holding hands while they read stories to the little kids, gazing romantically at each other as they passed out refreshments, disappearing among the dark bookshelves after the second-graders were asleep.

She swallowed hard. "Beth," she said seriously, "I can't go if Randy and Sara are going to be there. I have to take my name off the list."

Beth looked panic-stricken. "Oh, Jana, please don't," she begged. "You have to go. I mean, with Keith there, I'll need you. Who will I talk to?"

"Lots of our friends will be there," Jana offered. "Lisa's going, and Alexis and Dekeisha. You don't need me."

"Yes, I do," Beth insisted. "You're my best friend."

"But, Beth—"

"I really do need you, Jana. You know I can't talk to those girls about Keith. It's private. I'd die if they found out how I feel right now. And besides, what if he acts like a jerk and ignores me all night? I'd need you more than ever then." Beth fidgeted for a moment, then added, "And I'd be there for you, too, if Randy and Sara are together."

Jana looked into Beth's pleading face, knowing that Beth would be crushed if she made good on her threat to remove her name from the list. But still, how could she possibly go if Randy and Sara were going to be there together? "I'll think about it, okay?" she said softly.

Beth nodded, but Jana knew that no matter how much she thought about it, she couldn't let her best friend down. She was trapped.

CHAPTER

11

*J*ana lugged her sleeping bag up the steps of the public library on Saturday evening at six-thirty sharp and dumped it onto the floor inside the double glass doors. Then she went back to the car for her backpack with her overnight things in it and a plate of brownies covered with aluminum foil, which was her contribution to the evening's refreshments. Waving good-bye to Pink as he pulled away from the curb, she turned and went back into the library with a sigh. She tried to concentrate on how happy Beth had been when Jana told her she would come tonight and not let thoughts of Randy and Sara's being here together send her into a panic.

A sudden banging on the door startled her. Looking around, she saw Beth standing outside with her arms too full to open the door.

"Gosh, Beth," said Jana, laughing as she pushed open the door for her friend, "we're only going to be here overnight. You brought enough stuff to stay a week."

Beth dropped her sleeping bag at her feet and shifted the lavender makeup case she was carrying to the other hand, which also held a bulging paper bag. In addition, she had her backpack hanging on one shoulder and her purse dangling from the other.

"Keith's going to be here," she said, as if that explained it all.

"So?" asked Jana.

"Jana, what's wrong with you? He's going to see what I look like when I first wake up in the morning. You know, greasy hair, puffy eyes. In fact, I was thinking about staying awake all night to make sure I don't get too messed up. What do you think?"

"I think you're crazy," replied Jana, but instinctively her hand went to her hair. She hadn't thought about how she would look in the morning, especially after flopping around in a sleeping bag all night. Her hair would be dripping with grease, and before she left home she had felt the beginning of a pimple on the left side of her nose. It would be as red as a stoplight by morning.

How would Sara Sawyer look? she wondered. Perfect, probably.

"So I had to bring shampoo and conditioner and

my blow-dryer and curling iron," Beth went on, nodding toward her makeup case. "I know they don't have showers here, but I can wash my hair in the bathroom sink. Oh, and I brought my acne medicine and one of Brittany's cover-up sticks, just in case of emergency. You can borrow it if you want to. I see you've got a zit coming on your nose."

"Oh, Beth, you're too much!" Jana said, snorting in exasperation. "Come on. Let's find a place to put all this stuff before everybody else gets here."

Beth picked up her sleeping bag again and lumbered along behind Jana as they crossed the main room of the library and headed for the children's wing, where the overnight party was going to be held. Even though she wasn't exactly a child anymore, Jana still loved the children's wing. It had been added to the old building only a few years before and had a modern look, with lots of windows full of hanging plants, and a cathedral ceiling that rose to a high point in the center of the room. Along one wall was a huge hammock and several big overstuffed chairs, where kids could curl up with their books, and in winter there was always a fire in the fireplace. On the opposite wall was the most amazing thing in the whole library, a tree house. A huge old elm tree that had to be removed from the library grounds when the children's wing was added had been brought inside and set into the concrete under the floor; local parents had constructed a real tree house among its branches. It was the coziest place in the world to read a book.

"Come on in, girls," called Mrs. Hawley, the children's librarian. She gestured toward an empty corner of the room. "You can put your things over there for now and help me get set up. The children should begin arriving pretty soon."

For the next few minutes the girls were too busy for Jana to give much thought to Randy and Sara or greasy hair and sprouting pimples. They helped Mrs. Hawley set up the refreshment table and distribute craft materials and games to each of the small reading tables around the room. The children and their parents were pouring in by now, and most of the junior-high Book Buddies had arrived also. Jana tried to keep her eyes down so that she wouldn't look at the door at the wrong moment and see Randy and Sara coming in together.

At one point, when Jana set her plate of brownies on the refreshment table and Beth added her own platter of peanut butter cookies, Beth glanced toward the door. Suddenly she nudged Jana and said in a high-pitched, squeaky voice, "Oh, my gosh! Keith's here! How do I look?"

"Great," Jana called over her shoulder as she left Beth standing beside the refreshment table and raced to the tree house, where two boys were midway up the ladder, hanging on with one hand and trying to push each other off with the other.

"Okay, guys. Enough. Somebody's going to get hurt," she said in her most authoritarian voice.

"I was here first!" yelled the bigger of the two, lunging at the other boy.

"No, you weren't!" insisted the smaller one, who immediately hauled back his foot and kicked the bigger boy in the shin.

"I said, stop it!" Jana commanded. She reached out to grab each of them, only to find that now they were attacking her with their fists.

Before she could react, Keith stepped between Jana and the boys, grabbing each one firmly by the arm and drawing them slowly down the ladder. When they were standing on the floor, he leaned down and began talking to them. Jana watched in amazement. She couldn't hear what Keith was saying to the boys, but their immediate reaction was to drop their heads in shame, and she thought she heard the bigger boy saying that he was sorry. A moment later they raced off in opposite directions.

"Wow, Keith. That was terrific," said Jana in genuine admiration. "You really know how to handle second-grade boys."

Keith beamed at her. "Nothing to it," he joked. "Used to be one myself."

Jana couldn't help laughing. She remembered Keith in second grade, and he had been a holy terror.

Keith's eyes twinkled. "So maybe now you're glad I came tonight," he said. "Maybe we could sit over in the corner, and I could explain the secrets of stopping fights between little kids."

"All right, Keith, don't start that again," warned Jana. "I told you, I'm not going to date you, and that's that."

"Oh, come on, Jana. Just go out with me once, okay? Try it—you'll like it! I promise!"

"No, Keith," she said between clenched teeth. "Now leave me alone." She spun away and left him standing beside the tree house.

"What was *that* all about?" Beth demanded when Jana returned to the refreshment table.

Jana avoided Beth's eyes. "What was what all about?"

"You and Keith. It looked like a pretty private conversation to me."

"Don't be silly," replied Jana. "Those two little kids were trying to kill each other. Keith broke them up when I couldn't."

"Yeah, I saw that," said Beth. "But then you both hung around. What were you talking about, anyway?"

"Nothing . . ." Jana hesitated. "I mean . . . I complimented him on being able to handle second-grade boys . . . and, well . . . he made a joke about how he used to be one. Honestly, Beth, I don't understand why you're so paranoid."

Beth sighed. "Me, either. Sorry."

Jana felt like collapsing with relief. She would absolutely die if Beth ever found out that Keith was asking her out. There would be no way in the world that she could explain the truth to her best friend. It was too awful to tell *anyone*, even the rest of The Fabulous Five.

At the same time, she had the funny feeling that someone else was watching her. Looking up, she locked eyes with Randy, who was standing alone by the checkout desk on the other side of the room. He didn't move when their eyes met, and his expression was anything but smiling. Jana's momentary feeling of relief was replaced by a sinking feeling.

How long had Randy been watching her? Had he seen her talking to Keith, too? she wondered. And if he had, did he have the same suspicions as Beth?

CHAPTER

12

*A*t one minute until seven o'clock Mrs. Hawley announced that the countdown to the read-in would begin. "We'll read for half an hour, tally up our pages, and then go on to another activity," she said. "Okay, everybody. Watch that second hand. *Go!*"

"Fifty-nine! Fifty-eight! Fifty-seven!" The second-graders chanted off the seconds as they watched the clock on the wall above the librarian's desk.

The floor was a patchwork quilt of brightly colored sleeping bags, which had been spread out for each child and his or her Book Buddy to sit on.

"Thirty-one! Thirty! Twenty-nine!"

While the countdown continued around them, Jana smiled at the slender little girl with long brown hair and enormous eyes who sat beside her. The little girl's name was Megan, and she handed Jana the book she had picked out for Jana to read to her.

"But there aren't any words in *Good Dog, Carl*," whispered Jana, thumbing through the pages. "It's all pictures."

Megan turned her big eyes on Jana and said solemnly, "That's okay. It's a book, and our teacher said we could pick out any book we wanted. Besides, it's my favorite story."

Jana took a deep breath and tried again. "But, Megan, looking at pictures isn't the same as reading, and that's what we're supposed to do," she explained patiently. "Surely there's another book that you like *almost* as much as *Good Dog, Carl*."

Megan blinked a couple of times and slowly shook her head. "Nope," she said. "I want *Good Dog, Carl*." Then she crossed her arms and looked at Jana as if to say that the subject was closed.

"Okay, okay, I'll read the pictures," Jana muttered as the countdown ended and a cheer went up around the room.

The soft murmur of the Book Buddies' voices reading to their students filled the room as Jana opened the book and began telling the story to Megan. To Jana's surprise she was suddenly glad that the little girl had chosen a book without words. It meant that she didn't have to keep her eyes glued to the page the way the other Book Buddies did. Glancing up from time to time, she was able to spot

Randy sitting cross-legged on a bright red sleeping bag near the center of the room. His head was lowered as he read to a boy who listened intently and reached up now and then to swipe an unruly lock of blond hair out of his eyes.

Had Randy been watching as she talked to Keith? she wondered again. And had he actually been upset about it? Was it possible that he was worried that she might be interested in Keith? The idea gave her a small spark of hope. But then she noticed Sara Sawyer sitting on the sleeping bag beside Randy's, and she frowned.

"Come on, Jana," said Megan. "You're supposed to be reading."

Jana jerked her attention back to the book. "Oh, yeah. Sorry." When she finished the story, she handed the book back to Megan and asked, "Okay, what next?"

"Here." Megan pulled another book out of the canvas bag beside her.

"*Charlotte's Web*, huh?" said Jana. "That's a good one." With one last look in Randy's direction she opened the book and began to read.

At seven-thirty Mrs. Hawley blew a whistle to signal that it was time to stop reading. Megan counted up the pages they had covered and scurried up to the librarian's desk to give her their total.

As the second-graders streamed toward Mrs. Hawley, Jana sneaked another glance at Randy. To her relief he was just sitting there, looking around and not paying much attention to anybody. Curtis Trowbridge and Whitney Larkin were directly in front of him, and Whitney had stretched across her sleeping bag and was talking to Curtis.

Out of the corner of her eye Jana could see Keith trying to get her attention. Rats! she thought. Why can't he take the hint and just leave me alone?

"Psst. Jana!" Keith called.

Jana let out a sharp breath and was considering giving Keith a dirty look when she saw Sara lean over and tap Randy on the shoulder. Jana narrowed her eyes and watched Randy smile at Sara, and the two of them lapsed into conversation. Keith was still trying to attract Jana's attention, but Jana ignored him, unable to take her eyes off Randy and Sara.

"All right, everyone," called Mrs. Hawley. "Great news! Forty-five second-graders and their Book Buddies have read a total of one thousand two hundred thirty-six pages!"

A big cheer went up, and when the noise died down, Mrs. Hawley announced that they would all play a musical game for the next half hour to stretch their legs before going back to reading.

Jana avoided looking at Keith all through the game, even though she could feel him looking at her. When they settled back down to reading, Jana breathed a sigh of relief that for the next half hour, at least, she wouldn't have to worry about Keith. Megan stretched out on her stomach and propped herself up on her elbows as Jana picked up the story where she had left off.

She was just finishing chapter two when something whizzed by her face and dropped into the open book in her lap. Startled, Jana looked down at a piece of paper folded and refolded into a tiny square. Probably a note from Beth, she thought, telling me about her latest scheme for getting Keith back.

Megan was gazing off into the distance, listening to the story, and hadn't noticed, so Jana unfolded the note with one hand as she continued to read aloud.

The instant she opened the note, she was sorry. It wasn't from Beth, after all. It was from Keith! Even worse, he had drawn a big heart in the center of the page, and inside the heart he had written:

Keith Masterson
+
Jana Morgan

Jana stopped reading in midsentence, and she could feel heat climbing up her neck and spreading over her face. What is the matter with Keith, anyway? she thought. What does it take to get through to him?

"What's that, Jana?" asked Megan. She was leaning forward, trying to see the note.

"Oh, nothing," Jana mumbled. She folded the paper again and put it down on the sleeping bag beside her leg, promising herself that she would deal with it later.

This time the half hour of reading seemed endless. Jana tried to keep her mind on the story for Megan's sake, but too many thoughts jumbled together in her mind. Randy and Sara's looking so interested in each other. Keith's not taking no for an answer. Beth's seeming suspicious about Jana's talking to Keith. What could go wrong next?

Finally Mrs. Hawley blew her whistle again. Megan counted the pages and scurried to turn in their tally. Refreshments would be next, and Jana scrambled to her feet and eyed the table covered with cookies, brownies, and glasses of juice. She was more than ready for a snack.

She had hardly gotten to her feet when she was almost knocked down again by Beth, who had spider-walked across half a dozen sleeping bags and she grabbed the note off the floor as she jumped to her feet beside Jana.

"What did he say?" Beth cried excitedly. "I saw Keith pitch this note in your lap. Does it say he wants to get back together with me?"

Jana watched in horror as Beth fumbled with the square piece of paper.

"No!" yelled Jana. "Give that to me!"

Beth looked at Jana in surprise as she continued to unfold the paper. "But—"

"I said, give it to me!" Jana demanded. Her hand flew out, and she grabbed at the note, tearing it in half.

A crowd of kids was gathering now to see what all the yelling was about, and Jana could see Randy staring at her with a shocked expression. She couldn't react. Everything seemed to be happening in slow motion.

Beth was looking down at the two halves of the note, suspended in the air from their outstretched hands like pieces of a jigsaw puzzle. Now she was looking up at Jana, her eyes filled with pain. Slowly Beth's mouth opened and formed Jana's name.

"It says, 'Keith Masterson plus Jana Morgan!'" Beth cried. "How could you? You're supposed to be my best friend, and you stole my boyfriend!"

"But, Beth! You don't understand!" Jana protested. "I didn't steal your boyfriend. Keith's been asking me out now that I'm not going steady with Randy, that's all."

"Oh, yeah! I've seen you two with your heads together. And you tried to make me think you were talking about me!"

Jana grabbed Beth's arm and pulled her to the side of the room. "Beth!" she insisted, glaring at the crowd of kids staring goggle-eyed at them. "Everybody will hear you!"

"I hope everybody *does* hear me," Beth snapped. "I couldn't figure out why in the world you broke up with Randy, but now I understand. You wanted *Keith*! In fact, it was probably your idea for him to break up with me! Well, you can have him, and *I'll never speak to you again*!"

CHAPTER

13

*J*ana gathered her things and left the library before the others were up the next morning, making an excuse to Mrs. Hawley that she wasn't feeling well. She didn't want to hang around and have to face Beth again, much less Randy or Keith.

When she got home, she said a quick hello to her mother and Pink and went to her room, pacing the floor and thinking about her incredible fight with Beth. They had been best friends practically forever, and they had never had an argument this big before. Beth had whirled off like a tornado after her big outburst, leaving Jana feeling humiliated and totally alone.

"Of course Beth's totally hyper," she reminded

herself aloud, "especially when it comes to Keith. And when she saw the note, she was too upset to listen to reason. But *still*, she should know I would never do such a terrible thing."

Why hadn't Keith come to her rescue and explained the truth? Or why hadn't Randy stuck up for her? He knew what kind of girl she was. But neither of them had said anything. They had left her to face Beth's anger alone.

I have to talk to somebody, she thought a while later. She looked at her watch, amazed at how much time had passed. It was two o'clock on Sunday afternoon. Maybe she could call Katie and Melanie. They should be at home now, and if she couldn't talk to her friends in The Fabulous Five, whom *could* she talk to?

Jana curled up on the end of the sofa and dialed Katie's number. It rang only once before Katie answered.

"Hi, Katie. It's Jana," she began, suddenly realizing that she hadn't planned what she was going to say.

"Oh, hi," Katie responded, and Jana thought she sounded a little funny.

"So . . . how was your big gourmet pizza party last night?" asked Jana hesitantly.

"Wow, it was *très* terrific," said Katie, sounding like her old self now. "You should have tasted the pizza. I put anchovies and zucchini on it."

Yuck! thought Jana, but she didn't say it. Instead she asked, "How did Tony like it?"

"He thought it was delicious, even though he wasn't very hungry."

Jana put a hand over the receiver so that Katie wouldn't hear her giggle at the idea of Tony Calcaterra's not being hungry for pizza. Someday somebody's going to have to explain to Katie that everyone's not crazy about *très* gourmet food, she thought. She felt more relaxed now, so she said, "I really need to talk to you. I've got a humongous problem with Beth."

"Yeah . . . I heard." The funny sound came back into Katie's voice.

Jana blinked in astonishment. "You *heard*?"

"Beth stopped by my house on her way home from the library, and she told me all about how you broke up with Randy and then sneaked behind her back to get Keith. Frankly, Jana, I couldn't believe you'd do such a thing, but obviously you did."

"Katie!" Jana cried. "Give me a break! How can you possibly believe that? I'm one of your best friends!"

Katie didn't say anything for a minute. "I always had a hard time buying your story about wanting to test your relationship with Randy by breaking up and dating other boys. I mean, it just didn't make sense. But now it does. You had a secret crush on Keith, and you had to break up with Randy so you could go after him. I'm really surprised at you, Jana. Beth was your best friend, and she really trusted you."

Jana drew in a sharp breath. Maybe she should have told her friends the story about her father and her mother. No, she thought, that's private. Mom told me about it in confidence. I couldn't tell Randy, and I can't tell my best friends now.

Jana stared at the telephone for a long time after she and Katie hung up. Had Beth talked to Melanie, too? If she had, there was no use in Jana's talking to her. Melanie thought of herself as an expert on boys, and she had been horrified when Jana broke up with Randy, calling her reason ridiculous. What would she think now, if she had already heard Beth's side of the story?

With a sigh, Jana called Melanie's house. Jeffy, Melanie's six-year-old brother, answered.

"Edwards residence. *Mr.* Jeffy Edwards speaking," he said proudly.

Jana smiled in spite of herself. "Mr. Jeffy, this is Jana. Is Melanie there?"

"Yup," he said, and the phone clattered on the table as he raced off, calling his sister's name.

A moment later he was back. "This is *Mr.* Jeffy again. She said to tell you she's not home. Bye."

Before Jana could protest, the dial tone buzzed in her ear.

Jana replaced the receiver on its hook and looked around the room in despair. Beth *had* talked to Melanie—that was obvious—and now, just when she had thought that things couldn't possibly get worse, they had! Katie and Melanie had taken sides with Beth. And not only were she and Randy broken up, and Beth and Keith broken up, but it looked as if The Fabulous Five might break up, too!

Jana dreaded going to school the next morning. Rumors always spread like wildfire at Wakeman, and she was sure that anybody who hadn't heard about Beth's accusations by now would before the bell rang for class. It would make juicy gossip, the kind that would keep kids whispering behind her back for days.

She knew the instant she reached the school ground that she had been right. Nobody looked at her as she walked along.

She stopped when she saw Beth and Katie and Melanie standing by the fence. She had been automatically heading that way. The Fabulous Five met there every morning to talk and giggle and wait for the bell.

But what about today? Would they want her standing there with them? Would they even talk to her if she went over to join them? She had an awful feeling in the pit of her stomach that they wouldn't. They weren't looking her way, either, but she was certain they knew she was there.

They should also know that I would never stoop so low as to steal my best friend's boyfriend! Jana wanted to shout. *I shouldn't have to convince them of anything!*

She spun around and marched off toward the building, but she didn't go inside. Her shoulders sagged as she tried to decide what to do. She certainly couldn't go to The Fabulous Five's spot by the fence. Still, she couldn't help looking toward her former friends, and when she did, she saw that Beth was looking back at her with pain in her eyes.

Jana felt her chin quiver as she fought back tears. Maybe she should try one more time to talk to Beth. She wanted so badly to run to Beth and hug her and remind her about how strong their friendship had always been. How they had been able to tell each other their deepest secrets.

But just then Beth looked away.

"It's no use," Jana mumbled, and scuffed toward the door.

Walking through the hall, she heard the sound of someone running up behind her, and then Shawnie Pendergast called her name.

"Wait up!" Shawnie yelled as Jana turned around. "I need to talk to you."

"Oh, hi, Shawnie," said Jana. "What's up?"

Shawnie frowned and shook her head. "Honestly, Jana, I don't know what's wrong with you. Parker Donovan was going to ask you out again, but then he heard all the rumors about you and Keith."

"There's nothing going on between me and Keith," replied Jana, bristling.

"Oh, sure. Then how come everyone is talking about how you and Keith secretly planned to break up with Randy and Beth so that you could go together? All the boys are talking about it, even Randy."

"Randy believes a lie like that?" screeched Jana. "You've got to be kidding! Randy would never believe a thing like that!"

"Ha!" scoffed Shawnie. "According to what Craig and Parker told me, Randy said he heard it from Keith himself. Even you can't argue with that. Especially since Keith told him that you two had a date last Friday night."

Jana stared at her, dumbfounded. She didn't know what to say.

"Well, I've got to go. I just wanted to let you know that you blew your chances of going out with Parker anymore, that's for sure," Shawnie said, turning and trotting down the hall.

Jana watched her go, thinking that she didn't *want* to go out with Parker again. But Randy was another matter. Surely he couldn't believe the awful rumors about her and Keith's actually going on a date. He knew her too well. Shawnie had to be making it up!

CHAPTER

14

Jana didn't see Beth again until gym, which was the last period before lunch. Jana got her gym basket out of its slot in the locker room and headed toward the row of benches where the girls changed into their shorts and shirts for class. She was already in a grumpy mood from being snubbed by The Fabulous Five before school and from hearing Shawnie's malicious gossip, and she was certainly in no mood to answer questions from Tammy Lucero, who plopped her gym basket down beside Jana's.

"What's this I hear about you and Keith Masterson sneaking around behind Beth's and Randy's backs?"

Tammy had a catty grin on her face, and it took

everything that Jana had to keep her cool. Tammy was the biggest gossip in Wakeman Junior High, and the last thing Jana needed was Tammy getting on her case.

Just then Beth came into the room. "It's true," she said in a deadly serious voice. "And that's just about as low as anybody can get."

Tears stung Jana's eyes as she looked straight at Beth. "You can't believe that," she said just above a whisper.

"I can't believe anything else," answered Beth, her eyes locked with Jana's as they stood like statues facing each other across the room.

The locker room was filling up now as more girls rushed in to change into their gym clothes. Most of them glanced at Beth and Jana, and a few reacted by whispering or giggling among themselves, but there wasn't time to do much more than scramble into their shorts and shirts and rush into the girls' gym before the second bell.

The locker room was empty of everyone except Jana and Beth when the bell rang. Still, neither of them had moved. Jana's heart was pounding as she tried to project all of her hurt and misery through her eyes. Surely Beth would see how awful she felt and know deep in her heart that Jana could never do the things Beth had accused her of.

Suddenly the door from the gym burst open, and Miss Wolfe, the physical education teacher, strode into the room.

"Vy aren't you girls dressed and on zee floor?" she demanded in her thick German accent.

The spell was broken.

"Sorry, Miss Wolfe," Jana mumbled, unbuttoning her blouse and reaching for her gym shirt.

Neither girl looked at the other as they quickly changed clothes and joined the rest of the class on the gym floor. After the class was over and Jana was dressed again and hurrying to her next class, she couldn't even remember whose basketball team she had been on or if she had scored any points.

At lunchtime, Jana wasn't hungry. Besides, she didn't know whom she would sit with if she went into the cafeteria. Instead she pitched her lunch into a trash can and went outside to sit on the steps and think.

This whole mess was Keith's fault. Why did he have to have a crush on her, anyway? She didn't *want* to be his girlfriend! And even if she did, she would never do a thing like that to her best friend!

The more she thought about the lies Keith was telling, the angrier she got. When kids started drifting outside after lunch, she spotted Keith coming out with Joel Murphy. Jana jumped to her feet and watched as they headed toward the baseball diamond where the boys usually congregated this time of day. She clenched her fists as she saw him horsing around with Joel as if everything in the world were perfect. Well, it wasn't! Not only that, he was the one who had gotten her into this mess, and he was the only one who could get her out of it.

"Keith!" she called. "I need to talk to you!"

Keith grinned at her and then said something to Joel before trotting in her direction.

"Not *here*," she grumbled. "Do you want everybody to see us?"

"Sure, why not?"

Jana frowned at Keith and then glanced around the school ground. The coast was still clear, since most of the kids who had come out so far were eighth- and ninth-graders.

"Over here," she instructed, motioning him around the corner toward the back of the building. Kids hardly ever went back there because that was where the trash dumpsters were located, and they didn't always smell terrific.

"Who are we hiding from?" Keith asked.

"As if you didn't know." Jana spat the words back at him. "Listen, Keith, everybody thinks you and I have been sneaking around behind Beth's and Randy's backs. In fact, I've even heard that you're the one spreading the rumor. You've got to tell them it isn't true!"

Keith gave her a cocky grin. "Why should I do that?"

Jana drew in a sharp breath and exhaled angrily. She was getting more furious by the minute. "Because it *isn't* true! You know that! And nobody will believe *me*!"

Keith thought for a moment, his grin getting

wider. "I've got an idea. Why don't I come over to-night and we can talk about it?"

"*Keith!*" Jana exploded. She stepped forward, stopping so close to him that their noses almost touched. She opened her mouth to shout at him, to yell at the top of her lungs that she would never go out with him even if he were the last boy on earth. But fury bubbled up inside her and choked off the words.

Just then she heard giggling and spun around to see Tammy Lucero and Laura McCall peeking around the corner of the building.

"Will you look at the lovebirds hiding behind the dumpsters?" cooed Tammy. Then she pursed her lips and made little smooching noises.

"Riiiight," Laura said and nodded knowingly. "I guess those rumors must be true."

Jana stared at them in astonishment. She didn't look at Keith, but she was sure that he had a satisfied smile on his face.

How could I have been stupid enough to let this happen? she thought in horror. Why couldn't I have waited until tonight and talked to him on the phone?

But she hadn't waited. She had been too upset, and now Tammy and Laura would be spreading new gossip all over Wakeman Junior High.

Jana picked up the mail from the mailbox in the lobby of her apartment building as she headed home from school, not really expecting to find anything for her among the usual assortment of bills and junk mail. It had been an awful day, and she didn't need anything else to think about, anyway. But she stopped in the middle of the stairway when she saw the airmail envelope banded in red and blue among the other letters in her hand. It was from Christie, and the words PERSONAL AND CONFIDENTIAL were written across the bottom of the envelope in Christie's neat handwriting.

She took the remaining stairs two at a time and hurriedly unlocked the apartment door, pitching the rest of the mail and her books on the kitchen counter and heading for her room. She flopped across her bed and ripped open the envelope at the same time.

Dear Jana,

I'm sorry it has taken me so long to answer your letter. I needed to think about the situation between you and Randy for a while before I wrote. I hope that by the time you get this, you and Randy are back together and everything is okay again. But just in case you aren't, here is how I feel.

I think it's important for kids to go out with as many others as possible when they're just beginning to date. It helps them know what kind of person is best for them. I know that dating both Chase Collins and Connie Farrell has helped me, even though I thought I'd die when we came to London and I had to leave Chase behind.

But I also think it's more important that no one get hurt. You said that Randy really didn't want to date anyone else and that he said he knew how he felt about you. That makes me wonder if you are so determined to try your experiment that you are accidentally hurting Randy. I know you wouldn't do it on purpose.

Please write back soon to let me know how things are going. I'm keeping my fingers crossed.
Your friend,
Christie

Jana finished the letter and read it a second time through a blur of tears. She had never meant to hurt Randy! How could Christie even suggest such a thing? Standing up, Jana paced around her room. What was the matter with everybody? Why couldn't anybody understand?

The ring of the telephone interrupted her thoughts. What now? she thought angrily as she picked up the receiver.

"Hi, Jana. This is Randy."

Her heart stopped. "Randy?" she asked in a weak voice.

"Yeah. Listen, there's something I need to tell you."

He sounded nervous, and Jana bit her lower lip. "What?"

There was a pause before he spoke. "I'm calling to break the date we made for one month after the experiment started. That way you and Keith can start going steady whenever you want to."

"Randy! What are you talking about? There's absolutely nothing going on between me and Keith!"

"That's not what he says," Randy muttered.

Jana thought she was going to explode, and she couldn't stop the words that tumbled from her mouth. "Okay, Randy Kirwan, go ahead and break our date if that's what you want to do! I can see now that our experiment was the right thing, after all, since you don't care enough about me to believe me, and since you didn't waste any time getting a new girlfriend!"

"Sara Sawyer's not my girlfriend," he argued.

"Oh, sure. Tell me another one," Jana retorted. "I see you together *everywhere*. I guess I'm the one who couldn't believe the truth."

"Come on, Jana. Sara shows up everywhere I go. I don't ask her to be there. She's nice, but I don't like her for a girlfriend."

Jana exhaled and narrowed her eyes. Whom did he think he was kidding? "So what about the sleepover? Answer me that! I saw the list. You signed up together."

Randy sighed heavily. "No, we didn't. I signed up because you were going. I guess Sara saw my name, so she signed up, too."

Jana was silent. She wanted to believe Randy, but how could she? If she could just talk to him the way they used to talk . . . But somehow the words just wouldn't come out. Silence hung between them.

"Geez, Jana," Randy finally said. "Maybe the experiment *was* a good idea, like you said. I found out things about you I never knew before—like how *stubborn* you are! And maybe I would rather go with Sara Sawyer, after all!"

Randy slammed down the receiver, leaving a ringing sound in Jana's ear. Stunned, she stared at her telephone in disbelief. It wasn't just an experiment anymore. The breakup was real.

CHAPTER

15

*J*ana stood in the middle of her bedroom, staring into space and seeing nothing. She was drained of anger now. All she could feel was a terrible ache in her heart. After a while her gaze fell on Christie's letter, still lying on the floor beside her bed.

She picked it up and read it again, stopping when she reached the part that said, *That makes me wonder if you are so determined to try your experiment that you are accidentally hurting Randy.*

"Oh, no," Jana whispered. "What have I done?"

She let the letter flutter back to the floor as she stretched out across the bed on her back and covered her eyes with an arm. Was it true? Had she accidentally hurt Randy by being so stubborn? *Stubborn*. That was the word Randy had used to describe her. And he was right.

Deep down I knew all along that I really care for Randy and that the experiment wouldn't change anything, she thought, but I was too stubborn to admit it even to myself. I had thought up this great idea, and I was determined to stick to it, no matter what.

Jana took a deep breath and thought about Beth. I hurt her, too, she thought. It really was my fault that Keith broke up with Beth, whether I could admit it or not. I was stubborn there, too, and made things worse by not calling off the experiment sooner or at least talking to Randy. When I saw what was happening to my boyfriend and my best friend, why couldn't I just swallow my pride and do something about it? Randy and I don't have to date other people, at least not right now. Maybe later, when we're older and are starting to make plans for our futures, but right now we should just be having fun!

Jana's heart leapt, and she jumped up and raced to call Randy, but her hand stopped as she reached for the phone.

I can't do that, she thought. It won't do any good. I'm in this mess so deeply that it is going to take a lot more than just talking to Randy. First I have to get Keith to admit the truth!

*　　*　　*

Jana was waiting for Keith when he got to school the next morning, but she didn't say anything to him at first. She wanted a few more kids to arrive. Jana watched the slow trickle of students onto the school ground until she saw that the rest of The Fabulous Five were in their usual spot by the fence and that Randy was among the boys who had congregated with Keith near the gum tree.

Jana couldn't remember when she had been so nervous. Her scalp prickled as if a dozen daddy longlegs spiders were dancing on her head. But she was determined, too. This was it. It had to work, or she was doomed.

Taking a deep breath, Jana stepped to the center of the school ground and shouted as loud as she could, "Keith, I have something to ask you, and I want everybody to hear it!"

A surprised murmur rippled through the crowd, and kids slowly moved forward, gathering around Jana. She could see the puzzled look on Randy's face, and Beth, Melanie, and Katie were moving in closer. There was no turning back.

Keith gave her a cocky grin. "Sure. Ask away."

"There's a rumor going around that you're telling everyone that you and I were sneaking around behind Randy's and Beth's backs, and that we planned the breakups so that we could go out together. Did you really say that?"

Keith raised his arms in an exaggerated shrug. "Why not? It's true."

Jana was totally flabbergasted, and her eyes bugged out in rage. Incredible as it seemed, Keith was going to stick to his lies. She had never imagined that he would do something so cruel. *He's getting even with me for turning him down,* she thought. *He's doing this to keep Randy and me from ever getting back together.*

"It is *not*, Keith Masterson, and you know it!" She swallowed the bitter taste that had risen into her mouth and went on. "Did you also say that we had a date last Friday night?"

"Hey, how could you forget a thing like that?" Keith asked, strutting around and grinning at the other boys as if a date with him had to be a totally unforgettable experience.

All of the boys laughed at Keith's joke except Randy.

"Gosh, you'd better refresh my memory," Jana said sarcastically. "I can't seem to remember where we went." She knew she was grabbing at straws, hoping he would say *something* that would prove he was lying. So far he hadn't. She had been home alone Friday night while her mom and Pink went bowling. She hadn't even talked to her friends on the phone.

Keith didn't answer for a moment. It was perfectly obvious to Jana that he was stalling while he made up a story, but no one else seemed to notice that. The crowd was quiet, waiting for his response.

"We went to Mama Mia's," he said at last. Jana opened her mouth to explode again, but Keith raised a hand to stop her and went on, talking to his audience as if he loved every minute of being in the spotlight. "Jana didn't want to go anyplace where Wacko kids would see us because she hadn't figured out what to tell Beth yet. That's why we went to Mama Mia's."

Beth turned furious eyes on Jana, but Jana could only look at her helplessly. Her idea of calling Keith out in front of everyone and proving that he was a liar had backfired!

"We even hid out in the booth farthest away from the window to eat our pizza," Keith went on.

Jana knew she was defeated. There was nothing she could say that would convince even one single person that Keith was lying. She was so wrapped up in her own misery that she almost didn't hear Randy's question.

"What kind of pizza did you order?" he asked quietly. He had stepped out of the crowd and was staring hard at Keith.

Keith shrugged. "Large sausage with double cheese. So what?"

Jana's mouth dropped open. At the same instant, Randy grabbed the front of Keith's shirt and pulled him close. "You're a liar, Masterson! Jana didn't go to Mama Mia's with you Friday night! I *know* she didn't!"

Keith pulled himself free of Randy's grasp and

said with a smirk, "Oh, yeah? Just how do you know that?"

Jana's heart was beating triple time. She knew what Randy was going to say, but most important, she knew that he really did believe her now and that he really did care.

Randy put his hands on his hips and looked at Keith with disgust. "Because she doesn't *like* sausage pizza, even with double cheese. You wouldn't know that, of course. What you also wouldn't know is that she always eats pepperoni, green pepper, and mushroom pizza. She's got *good taste!*"

Keith's expression went rapidly from surprise to fear as the crowd began to grumble.

"Hey, so I forgot what kind of pizza we had. Big deal!" he said, scowling. "So I was wrong. Okay?"

"You were wrong, all right," snapped Randy. "And you'd better never pull a trick like that again."

Jana stood awkwardly watching the two boys faced off at each other, her heart in her throat, praying that neither of them decided to throw a punch.

Slowly Keith began backing toward the school building, muttering, "Big deal, big deal."

As the crowd began to disperse, Randy approached Jana. "Gosh, Jana, I'm sorry I didn't believe you," he said softly. "I know Keith can be a real jerk sometimes, but he really had me convinced until he came out with that stuff about the pizza."

"That's okay," Jana told him, feeling suddenly shy. "It was my fault, too. I shouldn't have been so *stubborn*."

Randy's soft laughter broke the tension, and Jana laughed, too. Everything was going to be okay between them now. She could feel it. "And I really loved your line about good taste."

"Jana." Beth's voice was quiet beside her.

Jana turned to look at her friend, whose eyes were glistening with tears. Katie and Melanie stood silently beside her.

"I knew Keith was a jerk sometimes, but I never dreamed he'd pull something like that," Beth went on. "I'm sorry I blamed you."

Sighing, Jana tried to find words to explain. "I suppose you can guess most of it now. Keith was trying to get me to go out with him all those times you saw us talking together. I couldn't tell you. I knew how much it would hurt you."

"You should have at least told us," said Katie. "Maybe Melanie and I could have thought of a way to handle it."

"I know that now," admitted Jana. "I hurt you worse by keeping it a secret, Beth, and I hurt you guys, too, by not confiding in you. I guess I was just . . . well"—she swallowed hard—"being stubborn again. I expected you to believe me, no matter how bad things looked. I shouldn't have done that. No friendship, not even ours, can take that kind of strain."

Beth rushed up and gave Jana a gigantic hug. "I just feel awful! I should never have believed those rumors. I should have known better. Can we still be best friends?"

"Of course, silly," said Jana. She looked at each of The Fabulous Five. "We're all still best friends. And, Beth, I'm especially sorry about Keith."

Beth's face clouded. "Yeah, me, too." Jana thought she saw Beth's chin tremble, but Beth sighed and said bravely, "Oh, well. I guess I can live without him. I mean, I've always known he was immature, and he's acted like a jerk *lots* of times, but . . ."

Jana squeezed her hand. She hoped with all her heart that Beth could find someone as wonderful as Randy. But right now, she knew, Beth hurt too badly to even think about anyone else.

"Hey, I've got an idea!" piped up Katie. "Why don't the three of us fix a *très* gourmet dinner for Jana and Randy to celebrate their getting back together. I've got some great recipes." Turning back to Randy and Jana, she continued. "Melanie and Beth and I could cook the food, set a romantic candlelit table, and then leave you guys alone."

Randy gave Katie a blank look. "What's a *tray* gourmet meal?" he asked.

"*Très*," Katie insisted. "It's French for very. A *very* gourmet meal. Don't you people ever pay attention in French class?"

Randy looked at Jana, and she knew what he was thinking.

"Thanks, Katie," she said. "But if you don't mind, we'll find a way to celebrate getting back together on our own."

Then she winked at Randy and slipped her hand into his, and they walked away together.

BONUS! Here is one of Katie Shannon's *très* gourmet recipes for you to try out on your friends.

TACO SOUP

1 lb. ground beef
2 envelopes taco seasoning mix
1 can refried beans
½ cup picante sauce (mild, medium, or hot)
4 cups water

In a skillet, brown ground beef and drain fat. Add seasoning mix and refried beans, mixing well. Add remaining ingredients and bring to a boil. Simmer uncovered for one hour. Ladle soup into bowls and top with shredded cheddar or mozzarella cheese. Serve with corn chips. Makes six servings.

Here's a preview of The Fabulous Five #29, *Melanie Edwards*, *Super Kisser*, coming to your bookstore soon.

"*H*ey, girls! Have I got news for you!" said Randy as he slid into the booth next to Jana and the rest of The Fabulous Five at Bumpers after school.

Melanie looked up in surprise. Whatever it was, it must be pretty special for Randy Kirwan to make a big deal about it.

"What?" asked Jana. "Don't keep us in suspense."

A sly grin spread across Randy's face. "I don't know if I should tell you," he said, slowly shaking his head.

"Randy, stop teasing!" cried Jana.

"Yeah, Randy," said Beth. "Don't be mean. Tell us."

Randy shrugged. "This is really big news."

Melanie opened her mouth to join the protest, but before she could utter a sound, Tony Calcaterra stepped up to the booth.

"You telling them about The New Generation concert, Kirwan?" he asked excitedly. "It's going to be murder getting tickets."

"The New Generation!" shrieked Melanie, jumping up out of her seat. "They're giving a concert? *Here?*"

The New Generation was her absolute favorite rock group. Their latest hit, "Super Kisser," had been at the top of the charts for weeks.

"Oh, my gosh," said Katie. "I don't believe it."

"It's true," said Randy. "Honest."

Melanie, Katie, Jana, and Beth began singing in unison:

> ". . . She's a radical departure,
> From the girls I've known before.
> With her happy face and spirit,
> A wild thing on the dance floor.
> Even though she loves to party,
> I know she loves me more.
> And I'm standing tall,
> 'Cause that's not all.
>
> She's a super kisser!
> A super super kisser!
> She's a super kisser!
> A super super kisser!"

"Can you imagine actually being there and maybe even being one of the girls in the audience who gets kissed?" Melanie asked breathlessly. "I mean, that would be totally *incredible!*"

Tony looked at her. "What do you mean? Girls in the audience get kissed?"

Melanie shot him a look of disbelief. "You haven't heard about it? When they finish singing 'Super

Kisser,' they jump offstage and run into the audience. Then they each pick one girl and give her a kiss." She sighed dreamily. "Oh, guys! I've just got to go to that concert! And I've just got to be one of the girls who gets kissed!"

Katie shook her head in disgust. "Melanie, you're the most boy-crazy girl I've ever met. All you ever think about is romance and kissing. If you ask me, someday it's going to get you into a whole lot of trouble."

Melanie stuck her tongue out at Katie. "Don't be silly," she said, and went back to dreaming about being chosen to be kissed by one of the members of The New Generation.

Will Melanie's dream of being kissed by one of the members of The New Generation come true? Could Katie's premonition also come true? Find out in The Fabulous Five #29, *Melanie Edwards, Super Kisser.*

Do you and your friends know the answers to these trivia questions about The Fabulous Five? Quiz each other to see who knows the most Fabulous Facts!

#16 In Super Edition #2, *Caribbean Adventure*, name the beautiful tropical island where The Fabulous Five spend their winter vacation.

#17 In book #17, *Celebrity Auction*, what does Keith Masterson squirt into Beth's hair?

#18 In book #3, *The Popularity Trap,* who is the mystery candidate who runs for seventh-grade president?

#19 In book #8, *The Runaway Crisis*, when Shawnie Pendergast runs away from home, where does she hide?

#20 In book #6, *The Parent Game*, what is Shane Arrington's "baby" for the Family Living project?

You can find the answers to these questions, plus five new questions about Fabulous Facts, in the back of The Fabulous Five #29, *Melanie Edwards*, *Super Kisser,* coming to your bookstore soon!

Here are the answers to trivia questions #11–15, which appeared in the back of The Fabulous Five #27, *The Scapegoat*.

#11 In book #11, *Hit and Run*, what does Randy Kirwan do to save Jana from being hit by a car?
He pushes her out of the way and is hit by the car himself.

#12 In book #9, *The Boyfriend Dilemma*, what is Christie accused of stealing?
The notebook containing the answers to the Super Quiz, the interschool academic competition.

#13 In book #20, *The Witches of Wakeman*, what is the mysterious curse that threatens to ruin the drama club's Halloween production?
An old superstition that says whenever the witches' "Double, double, toil and trouble" speech from Macbeth is spoken on stage, bad luck will follow.

#14 In book #14, *Seventh-Grade Menace*, who is the terror of Wakeman Junior High?
Geena McNatt.

#15 In book #15, *Melanie's Identity Crisis*, what surprising thing does Melanie discover that she has in common with her great-great-grandmother?
Being boy crazy.

ABOUT THE AUTHOR

Betsy Haynes, the daughter of a former news-woman, began scribbling poetry and short stories as soon as she learned to write. A serious writing career, however, had to wait until after her marriage and the arrival of her two children. But that early practice must have paid off, for within three months Mrs. Haynes had sold her first story. In addition to a number of magazine short stories and the Taffy Sinclair series, Mrs. Haynes is also the author of *The Great Mom Swap* and its sequel, *The Great Boyfriend Trap*. She lives in Marco Island, Florida, with her husband, who is also an author.